His name is

PATRICK DAWLISH

He is a very large ma   shoulders
that his well cut sui   nceal. But for
the broken nose,   an early battle
in the boxing rir   d be as handsome
as he is massive . .

He is always jumping in with both feet
where the police fear to tread. And no thief,
blackmailer or murderer ever comes up
against a tougher, more resourceful, deadlier
enemy than

PATRICK DAWLISH

Death in High Places, one of the Patrick
Dawlish series, is by John Creasey writing
as Gordon Ashe, of which there are now over
forty titles and many have been published by
Corgi Books.

Born in 1908, John Creasey died in June
1973. Overall, his books have sold nearly a
hundred million copies and have been
translated into 28 languages.

As well as travelling extensively, he had a
particular interest in politics and was the
founder of *All Party Alliance*, which advocates
a new system of government by the best
candidates from all parties and independents.
He fought in five parliamentary by-elections
for the movement.

Death in High Places

John Creasey

writing as
GORDON ASHE

CORGI BOOKS
A DIVISION OF TRANSWORLD PUBLISHERS LTD
A NATIONAL GENERAL COMPANY

DEATH IN HIGH PLACES
A CORGI BOOK 0 552 09384 X

Originally published in Great Britain
by John Long Ltd.

PRINTING HISTORY

John Long edition published 1942
Corgi edition published 1973

Copyright © John Creasey 1942
This revised edition Copyright © John Creasey 1973

This book is set in Plantin 10/10½ pt.

Corgi Books are published by Transworld Publishers Ltd.,
Cavendish House, 57–59 Uxbridge Road, Ealing,
London, W.5.

Made and printed in Great Britain by
Richard Clay (The Chaucer Press), Ltd., Bungay, Suffolk.

**NOTE: The Australian price appearing on the
back cover is the recommended retail price.**

DEATH IN HIGH PLACES

CHAPTER ONE

WHITEHALL WARRIOR

Captain Patrick Dawlish of the 3rd East Loamshire Regiment sat back in a dilapidated armchair, an empty pipe between his lips. His eyes were fixed, a little bleakly, on a hole in the toe of his left sock.

From a vast fireplace in which several bricks were missing, a thin wisp of smoke rose from what his batman, rather optimistically, had intended to be a fire.

Dawlish's eyes travelled from his toe to the fireplace with an expression of revulsion.

'Not a pipe to smoke nor a spot to drink—Lord, why did I have to be sent here?' he declared to the otherwise empty room. He brooded for several seconds, and then said more briskly: 'This won't do, I'll get frostbite, April or not.'

He reached over, and pulled a haversack from a nail on the door. Amongst the miscellany inside were several socks, and he searched through them until he found one comparatively holeless. As he finished lacing his boot, the door opened. The light from three candles flickered in the draught, and one went out.

'Shut that perishing door!' snapped Dawlish. 'Isn't it bad enough when it's closed?' He peered through the smoke towards the newcomer, recognising a red-faced subaltern of incurable good-humour. 'Oh, it's you, Kemp, is it? What's the news?'

'I'm afraid there isn't much, sir,' said Lieutenant Kemp brightly. 'We'll have to bed down for the night, there's no chance at all of getting over the hills. It's snowing, actually.'

Dawlish glared at him.

'No need to look so happy about it. How are the men?'

'They've built a fire in one of the barns,' said Kemp, 'and

they've found a whopping great saucepan. It *smells* as if they're making some kind of stew.'

Dawlish grinned.

'Bless their hearts. Try to get a mug of whatever it is for me, will you? Have you seen Carter?'

'He's pottering about in the barn,' Kemp assured him. 'D'you want him?'

'Oh, let him potter,' said Dawlish, mentally condemning his batman to perdition. 'We'd better see what we can do with the fire.' He went on his knees in front of it. A gust of wind sent a cloud of smoke into his face, but at the same time, as if by magic, a tongue of flame shot upwards. He stood up, wiping the tears from his eyes. 'Roughly speaking, how far are we from the nearest village?'

'About six miles,' said Kemp. 'I didn't realise Wiltshire was so desolate, did you?'

Dawlish shrugged.

'It's not Wiltshire, it's the weather. Or me,' he added. 'Kemp, I'm fed up with manoeuvres. D'you know how many I've been in this year? Nine. *Nine!* West of Scotland, east of Scotland, Westmorland, Yorkshire, North Wales—the lot!'

'I don't think they're bad fun on the whole,' said Kemp. 'I know this is only my second, and the other was only a local show, but they give us something to do. I say, sir, d'you think there's much chance of us being drafted abroad soon?'

Dawlish rubbed the back of his head.

'Well,' he said, 'I've heard nothing officially. There's only one thing that's certain in the movements of the regiment: *I'll* stay in England. Battalions by the dozen get drafted abroad, but not me. They must think I'll get homesick.'

'You can't tell me that's the reason,' said Kemp earnestly. 'Er—you don't mind me saying so, I hope, but I've read about you. Often thought I'd give years of my life to be with you on one of your—er—shindies.'

'If you *were* on one of my shindies you'd add years to your life all right,' said Dawlish, laughing a little grimly. The fire was burning now, even giving out a little heat. Dawlish stared at the flames, temporarily oblivious to Kemp's presence. He was thinking of the 'shindies' which had presented themselves to him from time to time, alleviating the deadly monotony of camp life for a few brief, dangerous days.

He thought of his friends, Ted Beresford and Tim Jeremy. Of Felicity, his fiancée, who had been involved as often as the others, and come out with colours flying. Felicity, a member of the A.T.S., was driving Whitehall warriors about in large cars, he knew; her last letter had contained some vitriolic passages to that effect.

Kemp interrupted his flow of thoughts.

'I just come in, sir, to make sure it was all right to stay here for the night.'

'What?' said Dawlish. 'Oh yes. I'd better do some reports, I suppose. Nothing's come in over the air?'

'Nothing, sir.'

'Well, well,' said Dawlish, 'not only perishing cold, but apparently forgotten.' He gave instructions for the placing of guards, and was about to add a plea for a mug of stew, when his batman came in, red-nosed and blue-lipped.

Dawlish did not like Carter. He had, however, a rather offsetting habit of doing something really brilliant when Dawlish had given up all hope of making him act with even average common sense.

Now Carter brought in a tin plate loaded with steak pudding, beans and carrots. Under the incredulous eyes of the two officers he placed it on a bare kitchen table, sniffed, and asked whether the lieutenant was ready for his dinner also.

'Good Lord, yes!' exclaimed Kemp. 'I'll be back in a moment, sir.' He hurried out of the room, while Carter assured Dawlish gloomily that he had happened to find the tinned pudding and vegetables quite by accident.

Dawlish chuckled.

'You have my permission to have some more accidents, Carter, plenty more accidents, if they get results like that.'

A little more than twenty minutes later Dawlish and Kemp were sitting in front of the fire now briskly burning; warm, fed and comparatively comfortable. Dawlish visited the barn, found the atmosphere one vast fug, received prompt and hearty assurances that everything was all right and, after a quick inspection of the sentries, had returned to the old farmhouse. The snow, which had started late in the afternoon and come down heavily, helped by a wind which reached gale force, had almost stopped.

Kemp and he were reading a page each of the *Daily Cry* when there was a tap on the door.

'Message waiting for you, sir.'

Dawlish thanked his stars that he had not taken off his boots again and went out into the night, climbed into the radio van and lifted the receiver of the radio-telephone.

'Captain Dawlish speaking.'

'Hold on, please. Colonel Cranton wants you.'

'Hold on,' muttered Dawlish, 'with both hands nearly frozen!'

He heard a rustling over the wireless, as if papers were being shuffled, while he tried to picture Cranton, a little, monkey-faced man for whom he, and most others who had worked with him, felt a considerable respect.

He wondered what had led up to this call.

The large office was warm and thick with smoke. Cranton sat at his desk, glancing across the room to a man who had been with him for the past two hours. Cranton had respect and liking for the Under-Secretary to the Home Office, who had told a story at great length and then asked for Cranton's advice; it was pleasant to be asked for that, and to know that it would be taken into account.

'Dawlish is the man,' Cranton had said without preamble. 'I think he's in Wiltshire, on the Southern Command show. Have you met him?'

The Under-Secretary shook his head.

'I've heard some odds and ends about him, Cranton, and I imagine he'll do. He throws his weight about a bit, though, doesn't he?'

Cranton's wizened face split in a wide smile.

'When it's necessary. He doesn't take easily to red tape, and is apt to adopt a "do-it-my-way-or-do-it-yourself" attitude when it's the only chance of getting results. Usually he gets away with it. Amusing fellow in some ways. He told me once that the big fear of his life was that he would be given a room here, with some red ribbon to put round his hat.'

The Under-Secretary smiled appreciatively.

The telephone rang and Cranton lifted the receiver, held on for a few seconds and then said briskly:

'Is that you, Dawlish?'

'Yes, and I'm perishing cold,' he was told in heartfelt tones. 'This is an open van, and it's snowing fit for the Alps. Who is that?'

'Colonel Cranton.'

'Oh. I'm sorry, sir.' Dawlish contrived to put a tone of surprise into the words, and Cranton smiled as he went on: 'All right, I won't keep you long. Just where are you at the moment?'

'Somewhere near Warlingham on the Salisbury downs,' Dawlish told him. 'We're bedded down for the night, I hope. The road's impassable for traffic.'

'Hmm,' said Cranton. 'Salisbury. Yes.' He paused and looked towards the Under-Secretary, who was leaning forward in his chair, suddenly tense. 'I'd like you to get to the White Hart, in Salisbury, by lunch-time tomorrow, Dawlish, even if you have to wear snow-shoes. Eh? ... yes, I'll arrange for orders to be sent through to that effect ... I don't yet know, but I think so.'

There was a different tone in Dawlish's voice.

'What kind of a show is it likely to be, sir?'

'I've no idea, yet ... yes, it could be done ... I'll see what I can do. All right, go and get yourself warmed up. I'll see you at the White Hart. Goodnight.'

He rang off abruptly, then looked across the office to the Under-Secretary.

'We think the trouble is starting from Salisbury, and Dawlish is almost on the spot. Do you believe in omens?'

'I believe in coincidence,' said the Under-Secretary. 'Sometimes. What did he say?'

'That if it's likely to be a big show he'd like to have his friends Jeremy and Beresford with him,' chuckled Cranton, 'and he even suggested it might be an idea if his fiancée could be there, too. She's driving Boodles, I think, so that will be easy.'

The Under-Secretary looked back at him quizzically.

'You believe in letting Dawlish have his head, don't you?'

'Well, yes,' said Cranton, no longer smiling. 'And if you had seen the man at work you'd know why.'

CHAPTER TWO

GATHERING OF FRIENDS

In a bedroom at the White Hart Hotel, Salisbury, almost under the shadow of the great spire of the cathedral, a grey-haired man with sharp features and the severe expression popularly, but often erroneously, attributed to members of the legal profession, pulled the bedclothes up to his chin and peered across the dimly-lit room to a woman sitting at the dressing-table. He could see her face in the mirror, but the subdued light robbed it of the lines which daylight would have revealed, making her look younger than she was, and almost beautiful.

Painstakingly, she was smoothing cream into her cheeks when he spoke to her.

'Are you comfortable here, Paula?'

She turned, her expression almost venomous.

'You know damned well that I am. Why the devil do you always have to move when I'm getting to know some decent people?'

The man smiled, without amusement.

'For one reason, my dear, to try to make sure that you don't make friends with the wrong people. For another, it's much wiser to move around.'

'You're as nervous as a coot,' the woman snapped.

'I'm older and wiser than you,' said the man quietly, 'although perhaps not much of either.' His smile vanished as he saw her lips tighten. 'Sooner or later we shall be suspected.

12

You know that, don't you?'

'Not if you keep your nerve.'

'And if you, perhaps, curb your thirst, and love of uniforms,' sneered the man.

'That's a lie! I haven't been tight for months. And what about the news I pass on to you. If I didn't get on well with uniforms, there'd be a lot you wouldn't know.'

'Crumbs of information, my dear, do not make a loaf,' said the grey-haired man sharply. 'Your sense of your own importance can be dangerous, too. Don't allow yourself to think you are a key-agent, Paula, remember even I can hardly call myself that. A key-agent,' he repeated, closing his eyes and folding his hands on the bedspread. 'I have progressed a long way. Do you know that there was a time when——'

He stopped abruptly, at a tap on the door.

'A letter for Mr. Mooney,' a woman's voice announced. Quickly Paula took the letter, then closed and locked the door.

Mooney, sitting upright in bed, snatched it from her. The atmosphere in the room had grown tense, with an expectancy that was almost fear; it was as if a third, invisible presence had joined them.

Mooney read quickly, and then let the letter fall. The woman picked it up, her eye running quickly over the written page.

A Captain Dawlish will be arriving some time tomorrow. Assess him, report at once, and then move from Salisbury. Further instructions will be sent to the Royal Hotel, Amesbury.

K.

P.S. Let Paula get acquainted with Dawlish.

The man in the bed had grown suddenly tired and old, while the woman's eyes glistened as she read and re-read the postscript. Yet in spite of the triumph she was feeling she did not gloat; Mooney's expression forebade it.

Within five minutes she had gone to her own room, next to his. Although they were registered as Mr. and Mrs. Felix Mooney, and both were married, it was not to each other.

13

When she had gone, Mooney re-read the letter, frowning. He thought: I wonder how he gets his information? I wonder why we have to leave so urgently?

Through the revolving doors of the White Hart went a man so large that there was barely an inch to spare. He was in uniform with three stars on his shoulder, and the receptionist had just decided that he was very plain indeed, almost ugly, when he smiled.

'Hallo,' he said. 'Do you know anything about a Captain Dawlish?'

'I don't think so, sir. Is he staying in the hotel?'

'I haven't the remotest idea,' said the large man, taking out a cigarette-case. 'He asked me to meet him here before twelve-thirty, but *he* always had weird ideas of time.' He beamed again, and the receptionist decided that she had been absolutely wrong in thinking him plain. 'I'll wait, if I may. I suppose I can get a drink?' he added anxiously.

'Of course, sir, the porter will send the order for you.'

'Good, thanks.' The large man went slowly across the lounge to a chair near the fire, lit his cigarette and appeared to go to sleep, although a lift of his finger brought the porter to him.

'Bass?' he asked.

'I'm afraid we're out of stock, sir, but we've a very good pale ale. I can recommend it.'

'Good,' repeated the large man. 'Preferably in a tankard.' He nodded as the porter went off, and then grew aware that two people were eyeing him with some interest.

One was a sharp-featured, oldish-looking man, the other was a woman of perhaps forty. She wore a little too much make-up, and her expression, the officer decided, could only be described by the word 'inviting'. He decided, too, that he was too tired to follow it up, for he had been travelling since two o'clock that morning from Norfolk. Only on the last fifty miles had the sun shone, and even then the snow had remained thick on the roads.

Before his beer arrived the doors opened again.

Another captain, nearly as tall as the large man but very

14

much thinner, entered briskly. He stifled an exclamation, and approached the big man quickly. The first arrival rose at once.

'Well, well, well! It looks like being quite a party. Pat's not here yet.'

'Have you ever known him early?' demanded the thin man in mock despair. 'Ted, my son, it's good to see you. What's up—any ideas?'

'I leave 'em to Pat,' said Ted Beresford, and stifled a yawn. 'I've been travelling since the small hours, curse it. You look so darned fresh that you must be stationed here.'

'Wrong,' said Tim Jeremy. 'I was in London, on a long weekend.' He winked. 'What about some beer?'

Beresford repeated the order, so that they were both drinking from pint tankards when Dawlish entered.

He eyed the porter.

'Whatever they're drinking, a large one for me, please.' He nodded pleasantly.

No one would have suspected that all three were close friends, separated by the demands of war which had kept them apart for the last six months.

Dawlish sank into an easy chair, adjusted the set of his trousers, and indicated to the porter that one of the others would pay for his beer; Ted did so, with some indignation.

'Talking of the weather,' began Jeremy.

'Let's not,' implored Dawlish, looking about him.

No one was within earshot when he drew his chair a little nearer to the table, and then added:

'I had enough weather last night to keep me going for a couple of years. Cranton dug me out of a snowed-up farm to come here, just as I'd decided to hibernate for the rest of the winter.'

Beresford raised an eyebrow.

'Cranton, indeed. That's how we were released, I suppose?'

'Did you ask for us?' asked Jeremy.

'I did, and for Felicity, too.' Dawlish paused. 'By the look of it he's on to something fairly hot, or he couldn't have arranged it so easily.'

'Also he has a high opinon of Cap'en P.D.,' murmured Jeremy with a gleam in his eyes, 'which means that the said

P.D. is going to be unbearably swollen-headed for the next few days. Seriously, Pat, what's it about?'

'I haven't a notion,' said Dawlish.

'No, don't try that,' pleaded Beresford.

'It's true. When Cranton came through I was doing my daily curse about being kept in England. He must have searched heaven and earth to find where I was. We were in the middle of manoeuvres. That beer's not bad,' he added, drinking deeply and, as he did so, looking over the tankard towards the woman known as Mrs. Mooney. 'Have either of you had any conversation with the lady?'

Without looking towards her, Beresford said: 'Only as far as her eyes can speak.'

'Like that, is it?'

'I'll tell you what, Pat,' supplemented Jeremy. 'I thought she exchanged glances with the old boy just as you were coming across.'

'I thought so, too,' said Dawlish. 'But it's probably an over-eager imagination on our part. We're apt to get ideas when we start on a show. Or,' he corrected, looking at his watch, 'what we hope will be a show. Cranton didn't give us a definite time,' he added, 'but said he'd be here at lunch. What about another?'

'Remember there's a war on,' said Beresford, 'if we have two now we probably won't be able to get one with our food.'

'We'll chance that,' said Dawlish, and raised a hand to the porter.

It was while the man was walking towards him that a loud crash came from outside.

The noise did not stop immediately. It was followed by the blowing of horns, and the violence of shouting voices, while the shrill blast of a police whistle added its stridency.

Dawlish moved.

Until the police whistle he had been sitting back in his chair; on the first blast he leapt to his feet and sped across the lounge. Before Beresford or Jeremy were out of their chairs, he had reached the porch.

He saw a saloon car on the pavement, the front of it, smashed out of recognition, jammed against the wall of the

16

premises near the hotel. Another, smaller car was lying on its side, and several people were standing by it.

Dawlish was less interested in the smashed cars than in the one moving past the entrance to the White Hart. It was an army machine, hideously camouflaged, and the driver was a girl whose profile was not only good to look upon, but to Dawlish familiar enough to make his heart leap.

Just behind her a policeman was running, but had little chance of getting on board.

Dawlish, in a better position, made a flying leap. He landed on the running-board, gripping the handle of the rear door to steady himself.

The girl glanced at him, drew a quick breath, then concentrated on the road ahead of her.

A hundred yards or more in front was a large car, moving at considerable speed.

As Dawlish manoeuvred to get into the seat next to the driver he was reasoning that she must have been just behind the cars when the smash had come, and that she had some good reason for starting in pursuit of the one ahead. The police whistle suggested that someone who should have stopped had not done so. These deductions were overlaid by satisfaction at the knowledge that Cranton had done his job thoroughly, for the driver of the car was Felicity.

'Fast work,' he said. 'Where are we going, darling?'

Felicity glanced at him again.

'After that swine,' she said. The word sounded all the more vehement because she rarely used abuse. Something in her manner, too, was alarming, but Dawlish waited while she went on: 'He caused the smash, Pat. Did you see the cars?'

'Yes. A bad show.'

'Cranton was in one of them,' said Felicity.

CHAPTER THREE

DAWLISH LEARNS MORE

Dawlish did not turn his head, but kept his eyes on the car in front. He had not known Cranton well, but had come to realise that the Colonel was one of the most efficient men at Whitehall.

The situation was obvious.

Cranton had been on the way to see him, and Cranton had been crashed. The only reasonable motive was that someone wanted the meeting cancelled.

'What is it all about?' Felicity asked.

'No one down here knows, yet.'

'I had a chit early this morning telling me to drive to the White Hart,' Felicity said. She swerved outwards to avoid a cyclist who started precariously from the kerb. Then the leading car turned left, and Felicity said nothing more until she had also made the turn. She went on: 'I didn't know that you'd be here, darling. Is it another special job?'

'It looks like it,' said Dawlish.

Felicity glanced at him fleetingly.

'So you really know nothing?'

Dawlish nodded. She was driving well, and the speedometer needle was quivering about the sixty mark. He knew that a little further along the road the speed would be unsafe, for there were twists and turns by the dozen.

He would have preferred to be driving himself, but like a wise man he said nothing.

She was a lovely thing, with a loveliness just short of beauty, and the power to make his heart leap.

He thought they were gaining on their quarry.

'Did you know Cranton was coming down here?' he asked.

'No,' Felicity told him. 'I left about half-past ten, and I was near the White Hart when he passed me.'

'Was he alone?'

'No,' said Felicity shortly.

Dawlish leaned forward, frowning.

'So there were others in the crash, too? You didn't recognise them?'

'No,' said Felicity. 'There was a man, and a girl. She was in the back, the man was in front with Cranton. She might be all right.'

'Yes,' said Dawlish.

He didn't really think it likely, for his memory of the chaos outside the hotel suggested that no one involved could have escaped lightly. He wondered, like Felicity, whether the people in the car ahead of them would 'try anything'. He had not yet grown used to the idea that something was on foot again, that he had been snatched out of the monotony of Army life in England in order to try his luck with the King's enemies who operated unceasingly behind the scenes.

The road before them was clear of snow, which lay in dirty heaps on either side.

A tractor drew out of a side road ahead of them, in the path of their quarry. Felicity's lips tightened, and Dawlish clenched his hands. It looked as if a crash was unavoidable, that the car which had already caused one disaster would be involved in another. But with a swerve which took it on two wheels, the driver ahead rounded the tractor and went on.

Within a hair's breadth of death, the tractor driver had lost control of his machine. It plunged into the middle of the road.

Dawlish unwound the window.

'Are you all right?'

'Not wi' any thanks to yon madman, I'm not!'

'I'll try to catch him for you,' Dawlish promised as Felicity, with barely an inch to spare, coaxed the car between the tractor and the hedge. But they had lost valuable time, which meant the better part of three-quarters of a mile. There was little chance that they would make up the lost ground. At Fordingbridge they stopped for inquiries but no one remembered seeing a large Talbot passing through.

Dawlish shrugged his shoulders.

'We'd better get back, my sweet. We won't do any good here.'

'You could ask the local policeman to put out a call,' Felicity said reasonably.

'I've no authority,' said Dawlish, and added: 'Yet. We'll get results quicker if we hurry back to Salisbury. Shall I drive?'

A few minutes later Dawlish was at the wheel, unaware of Felicity's secret amusement. He was not particularly worried because his quarry had escaped; it would have been almost too big a slice of fortune to have caught the car's occupants.

The chance that Felicity had been approaching as Cranton's car had crashed had been one in a hundred, although made more reasonable by the knowledge that both had been going to the same rendezvous for the same purpose.

That Cranton had conceded so promptly his request that Beresford, Jeremy and Felicity should work with him, suggested a matter of urgency and considerable importance.

Despite the circumstances, Dawlish felt buoyant and light-hearted. Felicity always had that effect on him.

He sobered up, however, at sight of the gang of men clearing away the wreckage in front of the hotel.

It was two o'clock when they entered the lounge. It was fairly crowded, but he saw at once the woman with the inviting eyes, and the older man he took to be her husband, both of whom were talking to Ted Beresford.

He rose at once, greeting Felicity with assumed surprise. It appeared that he had been able to get a room on the first floor, overlooking the high wall of the cathedral close. It was a bedroom, but a table had been set for four, and chairs were about it. As Beresford closed the door, he said:

'Tim's gone to the hospital.'

'How's Cranton?' Dawlish asked.

'Unconscious, but he should pull through. He had two passengers, a man and a woman. The man was killed outright, and I haven't been able to find out who he is. The girl was hardly scratched.'

'Thank heavens for that, at least!' exclaimed Felicity.

'Where is she?' asked Dawlish.

'With Freddie Blake's wife. Freddie's stationed down here, and she's staying at the hotel. I thought that was the best thing to do, a spot of luck on the whole. Goo-goo eyes was very anxious to help,' Beresford added, eyeing Dawlish thoughtfully. 'Odd, or isn't it?'

'I would think so,' admitted Dawlish. 'Who raised the eyebrow, you or Goo-goo?'

'She did. Fluttered about wanting to do this and that, asked the girl up to her room, and very nearly put me in a spot. Freddie's wife, I've forgotten her name, got me out of it when I told her I didn't want Goo-goo and the girl to meet.'

'Could I be told who Goo-goo is?' asked Felicity, drily.

'The woman I was talking to when you came in,' said Beresford promptly, while Dawlish went on to explain a little of what had happened earlier. As he finished, a waiter brought in the first course of their lunch. There was no interruption during the meal, and when it was over Dawlish lit a cigarette.

'At least they don't starve you here,' he said. 'I wonder whether I ought to go along to the hospital, or wait for Tim's report?' He lowered the window and peered out, but before he withdrew his head the decision had been made for him. ·

'Tim's coming,' he said.

'I can't help feeling we should do something about the Talbot,' said Felicity. 'It will be too far away soon for anyone to trace it.'

'It's too far away already,' said Dawlish, 'and I don't suppose for a moment that they'll retain the same number. We haven't got the measure of this thing yet, and we may barge into something we would be safer to leave untouched, if we move too quickly. What angle did you take with Goo-goo, Ted?'

Beresford grinned.

'Lonely soldier, on leave. I will be delighted to dine with her tonight. Husband suffers from rheumatism. Any friend of his wife's is a friend of his.'

'Not bad,' said Dawlish. 'What's her name?'

'Mooney.'

'His, or hers?'

Beresford's eyebrows rose.

'They're registered here as man and wife, and she introduced me to him as her husband. What more do you want?'

Dawlish grinned. 'The marriage lines. I may be wrong,

21

Ted, but I have a strong conviction that husbands, no matter how rheumatic, do not normally like their wives to consort with strange young men, attractive or otherwise, after a chance meeting. Anyhow we'll accept the *prima facie* evidence that they're Mister and Missus, and their name's Mooney. Have they been here long?'

Before Beresford could answer, the door opened and Tim Jeremy strolled in.

His uniform was torn in several places, and his appearance had suffered sadly from the moment when Dawlish had first seen him. It transpired that he had helped to get the injured from the wreckage, while Beresford had concentrated on Paula Mooney.

He told his story while he ate, and in its essentials it was simple.

The surgeon at the hospital had decided that Cranton must be operated on immediately, and at the very earliest it would be the following morning before he could talk. Tim had waited until the operation was over, and had then been informed that Cranton was likely to be in bed for three weeks, and convalescent for another three or four.

'So if we're to do anything we have to find out what's what from Whitehall,' said Felicity.

Dawlish patted her hand.

'We've already made a bit of a start,' he assured her. 'We've Goo-goo under way, and her husband. We've evidence of intent to kill, and we've a girl, young and pretty if you're right, who is bound to know something. What have the police been doing?' he added to Beresford.

'Not a lot,' hs friend answered. 'The usual inquiries, of course, and I told 'em you'd be here about half-past three. I thought you'd better have time to scram if you wanted to avoid them.'

'You gave them a description of the car?'

'I didn't. Some passers-by did.'

Dawlish leapt up from the table.

'Well, Freddie's wife is next on the list, and the girl. This isn't going to be so good,' he added, 'if the dead man turns out to be a friend or relative of the girl's. We'd better get it over, I think. You'll come, darling?'

Felicity nodded.

'We'll wait here and think up something brilliant,' said Tim Jeremy lightly. 'Or Ted could go down and get busy with Goo-goo. What's the betting that she's been a musical comedy actress?'

'Bet with yourself,' said Dawlish. 'What's the number of Freddie's wife's room?'

'Twenty-seven,' said Beresford.

In the passage outside Dawlish and Felicity walked slowly, neither relishing the coming interview. Room 27 was at the far end of the corridor on the second floor.

Dawlish tapped. There was a pause before a youngish, big-boned, red-faced woman opened the door. He recognised her as Lady Hermina Blake.

She was obviously relieved at sight of Dawlish and Felicity, and drew them in. The room was large and airy, for the window was down. Standing by it was a girl with her back to the door.

Before the brief greetings were over, she swung round; Dawlish saw her blazing eyes, her unsteady lips, her clenched hands.

'I won't talk to anyone, I won't! He told them, and they let him be killed! It's no use asking questions, I'll tell you noth-ing, nothing, nothing!'

But Dawlish thought the tears so close to her eyes were of grief, not anger.

CHAPTER FOUR

GEORGETTE

On Hermina Blake's face was an expression suggesting to Dawlish that this was not the girl's first outburst. On Felicity's there was concern for the girl. Dawlish remained stoney-faced, knowing that grief and shock had brought a touch of hysteria, that the girl was not herself, and that only something in the way of another shock could revive her quickly. Already she had told him much: a man for whom she cared had taken information to Cranton, and because of it, she believed, had been killed.

His voice was sharp, his words cutting.

'Where do you think that nonsense is going to get you?'

The girl stared into Dawlish's eyes, startled as he had intended her to be. Before she could make any comment he went on:

'What's your name?'

'Wilson, Georgette Wilson, I——' She stopped abruptly, and colour suffused her face. 'How dare you talk to me like that!'

Dawlish said: 'Please don't indulge in tomfoolery.'

'Tomfoolery! *Tomfoolery!*' She screamed the word on the second utterance. 'You heartless beast, you dare say that, when my father's been killed in front of my eyes! There wasn't a better man in the world, he's given everything to his country, everything, everything! Now they've taken his life. He's dead, he's gone.' She stumbled a little over the words, while tears spilled from under her lashes. 'He thought everything would be all right now, and then this——'

She stopped abruptly, and buried her face in her hands.

Dawlish had never heard a woman sob more piteously.

Not until this paroxysm had passed would she be able or willing to talk, and he had seen no other way, but the one of seeming brutality, to bring it about.

Weakly he sat down, pleased to feel the pressure of Felic-

24

ity's hand on his arm. He waited five minutes, ten minutes, before the storm of weeping began to fade. Hermina put an arm about the girl's shoulders, and led her towards the bed.

Georgette flung herself down.

Hermina towered over the girl. She was a deep-breasted woman, well-known as a promoter of good causes with a heart large enough to encompass the world, yet with an unflagging loyalty to, and love for, her husband.

Dawlish stubbed out his cigarette and spoke more quietly:

'I'm sorry about that, Georgette.'

'Sorry?' she repeated.

Dawlish turned to Felicity.

'Tea?' he suggested.

Felicity nodded, and went out. It was wiser not to bring a servant into the room while the girl was looking and feeling as she was.

'What do you want to know?' asked Georgette listlessly.

'Just what you can tell me,' said Dawlish.

Suddenly, unexpectedly, the girl began to talk; so quickly that there were times when her words ran into one another and were difficult to understand. But the gist of her story was plain and graphic enough.

Her father was—she did not speak once as if he were dead—*the* Professor Arthur Wilson, specialist in economics and adviser to the government. He had been working on post-war schemes. With other members of the government he had been developing a plan for the establishment of sounder economic relations between Britain and other countries. Georgette did not know much about the scheme; she did know that her father had always dreamed of it, had seen a vision of a new world much nearer perfection than that which the Nazi hordes had ripped to pieces on their march to temporary triumph.

There had been attempts to make him retire, threats that if he refused he would be killed.

Georgette had not known of them for a long time; she had only realised that her father was worried, that his health was poor, that his doctor advised a long rest. He had refused to accept the advice, and had continued working. There was one special task of which he was in sole charge. Just what it was

Georgette did not know, but she imagined that only her father had been acquainted with anything more than its broad outlines.

At that point Felicity came in with tea. Absently the girl allowed a cup to be put in her hands.

Dawlish went on quietly: 'He is in close contact with the government, you say?'

'Yes, of course.' It was clear that she still felt hostile towards him, but he was not surprised by that; the thing of importance was that he had broken through her restraint.

'Who did he correspond with mostly?'

'Lord Breddon.'

'He had a personal secretary?'

'Yes, several.'

'Could I have their names?'

'I'd better write them down,' Georgette muttered. She fumbled for a pencil and a used envelope in her handbag. Dawlish waited until she had finished writing, and then said:

'Did these gentlemen know about the threats?'

'Not at first. All of us did yesterday, when he told us about them. It couldn't be helped, I had opened a letter and read it. I was with the other secretaries—I do some work for him too—and told them what it was. Then father explained that he had received a number of them. This one was more—more direct, and he decided to tell Lord Breddon. Then, yesterday afternoon, we met Colonel Cranton, and he arranged to bring us down here, to meet a Captain Dawlish.'

'You wouldn't know why?' asked Dawlish.

'He seemed to think Captain Dawlish could help us. Are *you* Dawlish?'

'Yes.'

Georgette regarded him without expression for some seconds, and then shrugged. It was easy to understand that she was thinking that the visit to Dawlish had been the indirect cause of the tragedy.

Dawlish said quietly: 'What was in the letter, Miss Wilson? The threatening letter, I mean. Have you got it with you?'

'No, father gave it to Colonel Cranton. It didn't say much,

26

except'—she paused, then went on very quickly—'that if he had not resigned, or at least applied for leave of absence for six months, he would be dead within a week. A week! And they meant it, they did kill him! Why didn't you stop them?' she demanded fiercely. 'Why did you let it happen?'

Dawlish said: 'Everything possible was done, Miss Wilson.'

'Everything possible! If that was the best you could do I don't think much of it!'

Dawlish said nothing, but thrust his hands more deeply into his trousers pockets. After a short silence he asked quietly:

'Do you know why Colonel Cranton brought you to Salisbury?'

'Of course I know. It's obvious. All the letters were posted from Salisbury. But why didn't *you* know? I don't believe you *are* Captain Dawlish! What right have you to ask me questions? Who are you?'

'He's Dawlish, my dear,' said Hermina quickly. 'I've known him since he was knee-high.'

'That's all very well, but I don't even know who *you* are!'

Quietly Dawlish showed the girl his identity card, together with his papers. He wondered whether he would be wise to ask her what she proposed to do in the immediate future, but decided that it would be wiser to leave that to Hermina or Felicity. He stepped towards the door, saying as he went:

'Nothing will be left undone to catch the murderers, Miss Wilson, and I hope you'll help us all you can.'

She said: 'Yes, I'll help in that all right. I'd like to kill the driver of that car myself!' She paused, and then added bitterly: 'Not that *you're* likely to get any results!'

Her antagonism was growing with her bitterness; to stay would be to make it increase quickly and unnecessarily. Dawlish found himself unable to find words that would serve any useful purpose, and left the room.

Georgette's dislike was a disturbing thing. She believed that he had been responsible for the accident; or at least that he could have prevented it.

Jeremy was in the bedroom on the first floor. The table had been cleared, but left in position, and Jeremy was lying full-length on the bed reading an evening paper. He put it down

27

and regarded Dawlish blank-faced.

'What's the trouble?'

'One girl, badly upset. One man, sadly misjudged.'

Slowly Jeremy lowered his feet to the carpet.

'That's the worst of being popular with the girls, a rebuff hits harder. How is she?'

'She'll come through,' said Dawlish. 'She's got all of the right stuff in her. Name, Georgette Wilson, daughter of Professor Wilson.'

'Arthur Wilson, the economic chap?' Jeremy put out a hand for the *Courier*, and unfolded the paper. 'What an extraordinary thing, there's a paragraph about him here.' He searched noisily through the pages. 'Ah, here it is. It says he is suffering from overwork and is going into the country for a rest-cure. All right, if you don't believe me, read it yourself.'

He pointed to a paragraph which Dawlish read twice. It said simply that on the advice of his doctors Professor Arthur Wilson, the famous economist, was spending several weeks out of London, and that during his absence he would not be attending to work. Dawlish rubbed his chin after the second reading, and then said thoughtfully:

'We'd better phone the *Courier* and find out where they got that information. It might help. Poor beggar,' he added grimly. 'He's got his rest-cure all right.'

'And that's our man?'

'If we're to believe his daughter, yes. Go down and phone, will you?' He watched Jeremy making for the door without really seeing him, his mind working at high speed.

Salisbury's importance was now explained to some degree, since the threatening letters had all been posted from there. Cranton might have made the White Hart a rendezvous because of that, but the connection between Cranton of the War office and a professor of economics remained vague. The obvious contact was Lord Breddon, whom Dawlish did not know.

'Hermina will know him,' he said aloud, and then the door opened and Jeremy strode in.

'Not too satisfactory,' he said, 'they got the story from the Professor's London house. A secretary phoned, by name

28

North.' He handed over a slip of paper with a name and address.

'Hmm, Gerald North. That means we have to see both North and Breddon. You'd better handle North, Tim. The address, I see, is 31 Portman Square.'

'Right,' said Jeremy promptly. 'What's my line?'

'General inquiry, friend of Georgette's, just home on leave. You met her at some club or hotel, be vague about it, but size North up, and try to get a look at the other secretaries too. Good hunting, Tim, and be as quick as you can about it.'

'Reporting to where?'

'The flat. I'll be there tonight.'

'Good.'

Within five minutes the snorting backfire of a Bentley could be heard from the side of the hotel, and in two minutes more the car turned into the road, making for the centre of the town.

It was fading into the distance when Felicity entered.

Dawlish smiled at her, but her expression was preoccupied. It was clear that she was concerned over Georgette. She spoke as she was closing the door.

'She doesn't seem to have any close friends, Pat. She proposes to go back to the London house, but Hermina's trying to persuade her to stay here for the night. Does it matter one way or the other?'

'I just don't know,' acknowledged Dawlish, and he spoke a little testily. 'If Hermina can persuade her, she'd better stay here, I think. If not, will you travel with her?'

'Of course.' She paused. 'Pat.'

'Hm-hm?'

'You know Georgette has taken a strong dislike to you, don't you?'

'I'd gathered it,' said Dawlish drily, 'but I don't think it will do anything more than hurt my self-esteem, and I'll get over that. Is Georgette staying in her room alone?'

'Yes. We thought it would be wise to let her be alone for ten minutes or so,' said Felicity. 'We're all complete strangers to her you know. It must be a bit daunting.'

As she finished speaking Hermina poked her head round the

door.

'Hi! Hermina!' greeted Dawlish. 'You do know Breddon, don't you?'

'Fairly well,' said Hermina promptly. 'What about him?'

'What's he like?'

'Very benevolent,' said Hermina after a moment's thought. 'A little staid, perhaps. You'll like him, but you might get impatient with him. He's fond of hearing himself speak.'

'Oh well,' said Dawlish tolerantly, 'don't we all? And by the way, I'm not too happy at leaving Georgette alone. I think one or other of you had better look in on her.'

'As you say, sir,' said Hermina mockingly, and went out, while Dawlish reflected that it was a happy chance that Hermina had been at the hotel. Little else had worked out so satisfactorily, and the least comforting factor was that he had no official status. He had received official instructions to get to Salisbury, but none to authorise him to stay away from his unit for any length of time. Ted and Tim would be in the same position.

He was puzzled, too, by Cranton's choice of Salisbury for the rendezvous. On the face of it there was no connection between Cranton and Wilson; he wondered whether anyone but Cranton knew what the connection was.

'Deep thoughts?' asked Felicity.

'Dark thoughts,' said Dawlish, trying to force a lighter note into his voice.

'You haven't organised yourself yet,' said Felicity comfortingly.

Before she had finished speaking the door opened with a bang, and Hermina strode into the room, her voice raised to a pitch of puzzled resentment.

'She's gone. She's run out on us, the little ass. Don't stand there doing nothing, get a move on, do something!'

CHAPTER FIVE

LOST LADY

Dawlish was moving towards the door as Hermina spoke, and his first words followed hers with hardly a pause.

'Felicity, go to the car park and find out whether she's there. Hermina, keep watch from a window.' The last words floated over his shoulder as he hurried towards the lounge.

Beresford was talking with some animation to a woman whom Dawlish had not seen before. He broke off when he saw Dawlish, muttered a word of apology, and stepped towards his friend.

'Where's Goo-goo?' Dawlish asked.

'She went upstairs with her husband.'

'How long ago?'

'About ten minutes,' Beresford told him. 'Mooney had taken a telephone call a few minutes before.'

'What's their room number?'

'They've got two, but I don't know the numbers,' said Beresford.

'No one you've recognised went out of the front doors?'

'No. Look here, Pat——'

Beresford's curiosity found expression at last, but he spoke to the air. Dawlish had gone in pursuit of the porter.

'Porter, do you know Mr. Mooney's room number?'

'Number seven, sir.'

'Good, thanks,' said Dawlish. 'Mrs. Mooney's in Number eight, I suppose?'

'No, sir, six.'

By the time Dawlish had reached the passage Beresford was on his heels.

'Try six, Ted.'

He, himself, reached Room 7, and turned the handle. He expected to find the door locked, but it opened easily. One glance was enough to tell him that the half-formed fears in his mind were fully justified, for there were signs of a hasty departure. Drawers were left open, a cigarette burned low on an ashtray.

Dawlish half-turned, to find Beresford framed against the doorway, his face set.

'She's gone!'

'Yes, it appears to be a general exodus,' said Dawlish heavily.

'Of all the ruddy fools, I'm the biggest,' snapped Beresford. 'She told me the telephone call was from hubby's boy-friend, who couldn't turn up for the usual game of chess, and I believed her.'

'Take it easy,' said Dawlish with a half-smile. 'We've only just started, Ted. Have a look round her room, will you? You might find something.'

For five minutes Dawlish continued to search Mooney's room, but found nothing except for two handkerchiefs and the top of a pair of pyjamas in the linen basket. The drawers were empty, the wardrobe had been cleared thoroughly, despite the evidence of hasty departure. Frowning, Dawlish picked up the pyjama top. Automatically he felt inside the breast pocket. There was something there. With rising excitement he drew out a crumpled piece of notepaper. He unfolded it, and then read quickly, his eyes narrowing as the full import of what was written impressed itself on his mind.

A Captain Dawlish will be arriving sometime tomorrow. Assess him, report at once, and then move from Salisbury. Further instructions will be sent to the Royal Hotel, Amesbury.

K.

P.S. Let Paula get acquainted with Dawlish.

Dawlish drew a deep breath.

'Well, well. I wonder——'

He broke off as Beresford entered the room again, still frowning with self-annoyance.

'Not a thing of any use,' he said. 'Any luck there?' He spoke as if he did not expect good news, and his eyes widened when Dawlish held out the note.

'Make what you can of that, old son.'

Beresford read, whistled, and his eyes brightened.

'Good Lord, we've got 'em where we want 'em! The Royal, Amesbury.'

'Yes,' said Dawlish, 'but we must bear in mind that it *could* have been left behind deliberately, to get us moving in the wrong direction, though I doubt it. That's not the major point, however. They—or "K"—knew yesterday that I was coming. Presumably Cranton didn't make up his mind until last evening, so there wasn't a lot of time wasted.'

'Good Lord!' exclaimed Beresford. 'That looks like dirty work in Whitehall.'

'Could be,' said Dawlish thoughtfully. 'But it might also have come *via* Wilson and his staff. If Wilson was told by Cranton yesterday, as his daughter says he was, there's room for a leakage there. Tim should be getting some hot news from Portiman Square, we needn't worry too much about that at the moment. The problem is: did Goo-goo go on her own, with Mooney, or did they take Georgette with them?'

'What?' asked Beresford faintly. 'Who's Georgette?'

'Come on,' said Dawlish, gripping his friend's arm. 'I'll give you the yarn as we get to the other room.'

When they reached the room where he had left Hermina, Dawlish had relayed all that was worth repeating to Beresford. They were joined a few minutes afterwards by Felicity, a little breathless and without any helpful news. The Mooneys had a car, but it was not garaged at the hotel. An attendant believed he had seen a 'young lady' going out of the gates to the main road, but could not be sure.

Hermina had recovered her equanimity, but was not pleased with herself.

'If I'd thought at all, I would never have left her,' she said. 'I can't bear to think of that poor, silly child wandering about without anyone to help her——'

Dawlish shrugged.

'She was left alone for little more than ten minutes. Just before you left her, Mooney had a telephone call. He and Goo-goo went upstairs, and presumably saw Georgette, persuading her that she would be better off with them than with me, no hard task in view of Georgette's frame of mind. The Mooneys were all ready for a getaway. I wouldn't worry about it too much. The problem is, what to do and how to do it? When do you expect Freddie, Hermina?'

'Any time,' said Hermina, 'he can tear himself away from the golf course.'

'Can you get hold of him?'

'He should be back by four,' said Hermina. 'What's on your mind, Pat?'

'It's probable that the Mooneys have gone to the Royal Hotel, Amesbury,' said Dawlish. 'Georgette may be with them, but it's no use my going to find out, and Ted's too well known to the Mooneys for safety. If Freddie could take a look-see, with you, it might help.' He paused, while Hermina said at once that she had no doubt at all that Freddie would do anything which held a spice of excitement.

'Supposing we *do* see them?' she asked.

'The main thing is to get hold of Georgette,' said Dawlish. 'Ted could tag along behind you, and if there's the need for quick action, he could do it.' He looked at Beresford. 'Fix it with Freddie when he comes, will you?'

'If he doesn't come too late,' said Beresford.

'Wouldn't it be an idea to find out if we can get help from the Royal?' asked Felicity practically. 'You could get the police to ask the manager for information.'

'Yes,' said Dawlish, 'except that I'm not sure, at this stage, what we ought to tell the police. I think we'd better leave it to Ted and Freddie.'

'And me,' interjected Hermina firmly.

Dawlish smiled. 'Name Freddie and mean Hermina! Tim's gone to Wilson's home, and you and I can only try Breddon and/or anyone in Cranton's department. There are half a dozen things we can do first, however. Ted, will you find out whether any letters were delivered by hand to the Mooneys last evening? The one I saw couldn't have come by post, there wasn't time. Then——'

He was interrupted by the manager, who told him that the police were inquiring for him. Dawlish frowned in annoyance, for he had forgotten them. He ushered the others out of the room, and was alone when a man in plain-clothes entered.

'Captain Dawlish? I'm Superintendent Fowler. Very good of you to spare me a few minutes over this unhappy business.'

'Yes?' said Dawlish, raising an eyebrow; Fowler appeared to be very friendly indeed, and he was apt to suspect excessive friendliness from police officials. 'Sit down, won't you? Cigarette?'

'I won't, thanks. I'm quite serious when I say that it is a great pleasure to meet you, Captain Dawlish.'

'That's nice of you.' Dawlish's voice was reserved. He was not quite sure of the reason for Fowler's pleasantries.

Fowler gave a comfortable chuckle.

'There aren't many policemen who don't know of you, but not many of us have the luck to meet you in the flesh. You see, I know Woodley of Ringwood pretty well, he told me about the Cole affair.'*

Dawlish smiled, genuinely relieved.

'I had word last night that you would be in the neighbourhood,' Fowler went on quietly. 'I was asked to give you any help I could, although I've no idea in what connection. Anyhow, you can rely on us for anything you want.' He paused, and then went on: 'Was the accident connected with your business? I heard that you had gone in pursuit of the car. We sent a call out for it, by the way, but there have been no results so far.'

'Oh,' said Dawlish, adjusting himself to this new development quickly, and finding the depression, which had fallen after Georgette's disappearance, lifting considerably. 'Who sent word to you, Superintendent?'

'It came from the Yard.'

'You don't know any more than that?'

'I'm afraid not,' said Fowler, and for the first time he appeared puzzled. 'Don't you?'

Dawlish raised a hand to his head.

'Precious little,' he admitted, and gave Fowler a brief resumé of what had happened. The narration took a little over five minutes, and when it was finished Fowler rubbed his chin in a rather bewildered way.

* *Murder Most Foul* by Gordon Ashe.

'Hmm. It hasn't been easy for you, yet, has it? How can I help?'

'You can get the Amesbury police to watch the Royal,' said Dawlish, 'and get all the information possible about the Mooneys. If you could locate Miss Wilson, or the Mooneys, it would be a considerable help.'

'You want Miss Wilson pulled in?'

'If I can make reasonably sure she's all right, it'll be better to let her have a free rein,' said Dawlish thoughtfully. 'Oh, another thing. Major and Lady Blake will be going to Amesbury, with Captain Beresford. You might ask the Amesbury people to let them have plenty of latitude, will you?'

'I'd like descriptions,' said Fowler.

'In a few minutes you can see them for yourself,' promised Dawlish. 'Have you heard from the hospital?'

'I've just come from there. Colonel Cranton is still unconscious. I'm afraid there's no chance of getting him to talk until tomorrow at the earliest.'

Dawlish shrugged.

'I'd a sneaking hope, no more. Well, I want to get to London. I must see Breddon as soon as possible, and I'll have a word with the Yard.' He paused. 'It mightn't be a bad idea if I phoned them,' he went on. 'There's nothing else you want from me?'

'You didn't see the accident, did you?'

'No.'

'Then I needn't worry you for a statement,' said Fowler, 'although I would like one from Miss Deverall. There's no hurry, the inquest won't be until the day after tomorrow.' Fowler stood up and accompanied Dawlish downstairs.

Dawlish watched him push his way through the swing doors, then went into the telephone booth near the stairs. He called the Scotland Yard number, thinking as he did so of Chief Inspector Trivett, whom he knew well, and wondering if Trivett had any information about the job which appeared to be known to everyone except himself.

He was speaking to Trivett within a few minutes, and from the latter's manner gathered that the call was not unexpected.

The Chief Inspector had a pleasant, rather crisp voice,

which came clearly over the wire.

'Hallo, Pat, how are you? . . . Good. I've something that I think affects you, but I don't yet know how. Lord Breddon died this morning . . . yes, Breddon. Don't bellow, you nearly deafened me. What's that?'

Dawlish said clearly: 'I'm asking you if Breddon's death was due to natural causes, or whether there was any funny business?'

CHAPTER SIX

LONDON TOWN

Trivett was vague about the possibility of foul play. The reason he had been quick to inform Dawlish of the death was that he knew of the Wilson–Breddon connection. He also knew that Dawlish was being posted to the Wilson affair.

'How much more do you know?' asked Dawlish hopefully.

'Virtually nothing,' Trivett assured him.

'I don't know whether the whole world is united in conspiracy against me,' said Dawlish with a scowl, 'or whether it's just an accident that everyone knows more about it than I do. I suppose what you're trying to tell me is that you won't talk about it on the phone?'

'I tell you I know nothing else,' insisted Trivett.

'Then how the blazes did you know what I was doing?'

'That's easy. We had instructions from the War Office to help you in every way we could. I think they came from Colonel Cranton.'

'Hmm. Well, will you try to pick up anything you can about (1) Georgette Wilson, (2) Gerald North, Wilson's secretary or any one of them, (3) a man calling himself Felix Mooney and (4) a woman calling herself his wife. The last two probably go from hotel to hotel, and they've been staying here at the White Hart for some time.'

'It would help if I knew what they looked like,' said Trivett drily.

Dawlish gave what descriptions he could, and rang off. But he did not immediately join the others. He was keenly aware of the fact that things had happened too fast for him to get a good view of them, and conscious of the ease with which he could make a serious mistake. He was puzzled over the whole affair, and because of it he was not happy.

Felicity was sitting alone when he went upstairs.

He bent down and kissed her.

She looked up with a smile.

'Well, what now?' she asked.

'London town,' said Dawlish, 'and probably some interviews which won't be as successful as I'd like.'

Felicity said, a little sadly: 'It's useless to try and alter you, and if I managed it I'd probably wish I hadn't.'

Dawlish's eyes creased at the corners.

'You're probably right; but this time I had no option, you'll grant me that.'

As they went downstairs to the car, both were thinking, from different angles, of these, to her, too frequent adventures, which meant that for a matter of days or of weeks she was constantly on edge, lest he be injured or killed.

It had been after the previous affair that she had decided to join the A.T.S. Dawlish had been a little uneasy when he had first heard of her decision, but in the end he had accepted it, as she had accepted his more dangerous excursions.

Dawlish drove at a good speed. Felicity knew that he was preoccupied, and doubted whether he was still thinking of her, but deliberately she allowed the silence to continue. She found her mind drifting from Georgette Wilson to the woman they called Goo-goo, and to the letter which Dawlish had found. That was a disquieting piece of evidence; even before Dawlish had known of it himself, a third party had learned that he was likely to be at the White Hart.

It was not the only disturbing factor.

The more she pondered it, the more the accident to Cranton, and the death of Wilson, worried her. Deliberate and ruthless, it suggested that the killers had known it to be essential that Wilson should not live long enough to tell the authorities of the plan on which he had been working.

At heart, she knew, her greatest anxiety was the knowledge that Dawlish was now a marked man.

Nearing Staines, he drew a deep breath, breaking a twenty minutes' silence.

'I think we'll see Trivett first. Do you want to come along?'

'Why don't you bring him to the flat?' Felicity asked.

'Not a bad idea. I'll ring up and try and fix it.'

Trivett, however, was out, but Detective Sergeant Munk, his chief *aide*, promised in a somewhat gruff voice devoid of approval to pass on a message. Dawlish, leaving the telephone kiosk, rejoined Felicity and, a little more than forty minutes later, was opening the door of his flat.

It was on the second floor of 88g Jermyn Street, and belonged, actually, to Tim Jeremy. Since Dawlish and Beresford had given up their apartments on being called up, all four friends now used it when on leave, leaving the smaller room for Felicity.

Dawlish went in first.

He said nothing, but Felicity knew that he had in mind the possibility that a stranger would be here. She felt her heart beating fast as he went forward, a hand at his holster.

The flat however appeared to be empty, the rooms carrying that forlorn air of those untenanted for some time.

Dawlish lit a cigarette, and smiled down at Felicity.

'Nothing amiss here, anyhow.' He looked at his watch. 'Nearly seven-fifteen, I told Trivett half-past.' He paused. 'Things are very quiet, darling. Suspiciously quiet. No one had a go at us on the road, and we weren't followed.'

'Don't sound so disappointed,' said Felicity. 'I'm relieved. I wonder——'

She stopped abruptly.

There was a ring at the front door bell, and the sound was so sharp and unexpected that it made her jump. Dawlish stepped towards the door, but she saw that he put his hand near his gun again.

His tall figure hid whoever was there. Listening, she heard a man's voice which she did not recognise.

It was deep and throaty, with a harsh note she did not like. 'I wish to see Captain Dawlish, please.'

'As you are doing,' said Dawlish, and moved to one side.

'You are Dawlish?' The throaty voice sounded surprised.

'Certainly.'

The door closed, and Dawlish switched on the light. In it he was able to see his visitor more clearly. Short and swarthy, the man had heavy, possibly foreign features.

Felicity disliked him on sight.

Before he spoke again the caller drew out a wallet, and from it selected a card. He handed it to Dawlish with a little flourish, and Dawlish read:

> Mr. Simon J. Simon
> The Aliens' Club
> London, S.W.1.

He said with no marked enthusiasm: 'I'm very glad to see you, Mr. Simon.'

'It is good of you to say so, Captain. This visit, so unexpected—I have not called at an inconvenient time, I trust?'

'Not at all,' murmured Dawlish.

'I am glad,' said Simon fervently. He hesitated, then said: 'May I remove my coat? I have been hurrying, and I am a little warm.'

'Let me help you with it,' said Dawlish. He was puzzled and intrigued. 'Will you have a drink, Mr. Simon?'

'No, please! I do not drink.' As Dawlish lifted a half-full bottle of sherry Simon added sharply: 'Captain Dawlish, do you not wonder why I have called?'

Dawlish said blandly: 'Presumably with a purpose which I shall learn in good time. Are you sure you won't have a drink?'

'No, no! I did not come here to drink, Captain, I came here on a matter of extreme gravity.' There was something in Simon's voice which gave the impression that he was used to wielding authority.

'If I knew anything about it I could judge its seriousness,' Dawlish answered.

Simon barked: '*If* you knew!'

'That's what I said,' Dawlish assured him.

'This is absurd!' shouted Simon. 'I am being insulted, I will not permit it! You expected me, you were advised that I would be coming to see you, and you knew on what subject.'

Dawlish finished pouring a glass of sherry, and then carried it to Felicity, saying:

'I'm afraid you've got the wrong Dawlish, Mr. Simon. I have no idea what you want, and I certainly didn't expect you.'

'Didn't Mr. Simon say himself that the visit was unexpected?' Felicity put in.

'Of course I did!' rapped Simon. 'It was arranged that I should commence like that, so that you could have no doubt as to my identity. Am I right in assuming, then, that you did *not* expect me? That you have *not* been warned of my coming?'

'Quite right,' said Dawlish, firmly.

'I appeal to you once more, Captain,' cried Simon. 'Are you *sure*? Or is your attitude adopted because you have some doubt as to my identity? If so, make what demand you wish for me to prove that I *am* Simon J. Simon.' He paused, and then delved into his breast pocket. 'My passport, my identification papers—here!' He waved the passport towards Dawlish, while the latter saw little beads of perspiration gathering on the man's upper lip and forehead.

Dawlish said: 'I don't doubt your identity, Mr. Simon, I just had no idea that you were coming. Who sent you?'

'Sent me!' snapped Simon. 'You mean, who asked me to come? I will remind you that I am doing this at great personal risk, I cannot understand the failure, I—who asked me to come?' He paused in bewilderment, and then went on abruptly: 'Colonel Cranton, of course. Are you going to tell me that you do not know him?'

CHAPTER SEVEN

MR. SIMON TALKS

Dawlish looked at the man for some seconds, and then said abruptly: 'Yes, I know Colonel Cranton. I had an appointment with him earlier in the day, but he was unable to keep it.'

Simon stared, his eyes growing more protuberant.

'*Unable* to keep it? An appointment of such importance!'

'It was unavoidable,' said Dawlish.

Simon drew back. The expression which suddenly faced Dawlish could have been fear.

'Unavoidable! Dawlish! Tell me! Is Cranton dead?'

'No,' said Dawlish promptly.

'I—I see,' said Simon, and passed a hand over his forehead. 'You frightened me, you made me think that he was yet another victim. Breddon—you have heard of Breddon?'

Dawlish said: 'Yes. How did you know?'

'It is in the evening papers,' said Simon, blinking rapidly. 'I understand more now. I was completely at a loss, you must realise, I believed you had been warned of my coming. At my suggestion Colonel Cranton was to tell you of a number of sentences, ones I would use so that there could be no doubt of my authenticity. It is impossible to be too careful.'

Dawlish said: 'Supposing you tell me what you told Colonel Cranton, Mr. Simon? And anything else that might be relevant. I had instructions from him to work on the matter which concerned Lord Breddon.'

'At least that was done,' said Simon more easily. 'Captain Dawlish, I have often worked with Colonel Cranton. I cannot go into details, it would take too long. I can say that I was instrumental in informing him of the possible danger to Professor Wilson. Have you seen the Professor?'

'No,' said Dawlish.

'He was prevented from meeting you, also?'

'Yes.'

'Dawlish, please! You are not being frank. What happened

to prevent your meeting?'

'There was an accident on the road,' said Dawlish.

'I—I am at a loss,' said Simon, with unexpected simplicity. 'Was the accident deliberate, may I ask?'

'It could have been.'

'Yes, yes, it could have been! But was it? You are not being frank with me, I would like the whole story, please!'

'Mine for yours,' said Dawlish equably.

'I must insist——' began Simon, but he was stopped by the ringing of the door bell.

An expression of annoyance showed for a moment on his face, but was gone quickly. Dawlish hesitated, then walked towards the hall. Felicity slipped ahead of him, and Dawlish was glad that he was left with Simon. He was intrigued by the gentleman from the Aliens' Club, and by no means convinced of his *bona fides*; he was not a man Dawlish wanted to leave alone, although he knew that Simon might have told the truth in every detail.

Voices sounded from the front door, one of them heralding the tall, clean-cut-looking man who entered.

'Hallo, Bill. Mr. Simon, this is Chief Inspector Trivett. Bill, Mr. Simon J. Simon.'

Simon bowed; Trivett inclined his head. Dawlish watched both men, wondering whether they had met before. Trivett's face was expressionless, while Simon regarded the other with a curiosity which he did not try to conceal.

'A pleasure to meet one of London's famous policemen, Inspector,' he murmured.

'Mr. Simon is a friend of Colonel Cranton's,' Dawlish added.

'I would hardly presume that far,' put in Simon hastily, 'though I am happy to have worked with the Colonel on occasions. I have just learned, Inspector, that he has met with an accident. I am grieved. I had arranged to meet him here, with Captain Dawlish.'

'I see,' said Trivett, woodenly.

'As that is now impossible, I fear that there is no need for me to take up more of Captain Dawlish's time,' said Simon. 'Good evening, Mr. Dawlish, good evening, Inspector.' He bowed again, and turned towards the door. 'Goodnight, Miss Deverall.'

Dawlish followed him from the room, and a moment later Felicity and Trivett heard the front door shut with a loud bang. Two seconds passed and it opened again, so quietly that they could barely hear it.

'What the devil is he up to?' whispered Trivett.

'We'll have to wait and see,' said Felicity, 'but I could make a fairly obvious guess that he is following our late visitor.' She pushed back a tendril of hair, and smiled at Trivett. Her expression told the Inspector that she was worried by Dawlish's manoeuvre. 'Will you have a drink?'

'I don't know whether I ought to follow *him*,' Trivett said.

'I should stay. He knows what he's about.' Felicity poured out a drink with a fairly steady hand. 'His quietness can be a little uncanny at times. I've never known anyone else move like it.'

Trivett took the glass with murmured thanks.

'What's it about?'

Briefly Felicity gave him a *resumé* of the conversation with Simon J. Simon. Trivett wrinkled his nose, then rubbed a finger along his clipped moustache. Long-limbed, dark, brisk in movement and speech, he was a likeable man; Felicity knew that, knowing too that although he often disagreed with Dawlish he was second to none in his appreciation of those peculiar, even intuitive qualities which made Dawlish so unusual a man.

'There isn't much in that, yet,' Trivett said. 'We can't prove whether Simon's lying, or whether he's told the truth. I've been in touch with Salisbury,' he added. 'Cranton's still unconscious, his reaction to the operation isn't too good.'

'Does that mean he's not likely to recover?'

'The hospital people were non-committal,' said Trivett. 'I wish I knew more about this affair, Felicity. I only know that Cranton was busy on something connected with Professor Wilson, and——'

'You'd better keep it until Pat gets back,' said Felicity. 'It'll save you going over the same ground twice. I wish he'd hurry.'

She looked at her watch, seeing that Dawlish had been gone

for nearly a quarter of an hour. It was this waiting which she always hated. She could not rid herself of the fear that one day Dawlish would not come back, or would return badly injured.

'Supposing you tell me what happened your end,' suggested Trivett.

Felicity knew there was nothing which Dawlish would want concealed from the police. Trivett nodded appreciatively from time to time, as she went over the past events. By the time she had finished, another twenty minutes had gone, and still there was no sign of Dawlish.

Meanwhile, Dawlish had reached the street to find the darkness relieved by the light of a crescent moon. Simon appeared to have no suspicion of being followed. He walked briskly towards the end of Jermyn Street, then turned towards the Circus and descended a subway.

Dawlish followed.

Standing well back in shadow he saw Simon approach a ticket machine. Hurriedly Dawlish followed his example, and reached the top of the first flight of the escalator as Simon reached the bottom.

Dawlish heard a train approaching, and quickened his step. Reaching the platform he hesitated; if Simon turned he could not fail to see him. He took the chance, and won. Simon boarded the train without looking round.

Dawlish stepped into the next carriage.

At Waterloo Simon alighted. Dawlish went after him, following as closely as he dared.

The final flight, leading to the main station at Waterloo, was badly lighted. Men and women faded into shadows, and it was difficult to identify one from another. By then Dawlish was four places behind Simon in the line of people on the moving stairs.

Simon reached the top, and stepped off.

The woman behind him did the same, and then Dawlish saw a shadowy figure move towards the head of the staircase, and heard a shout from the man in front of him. It was impossible to see what happened, but without further warning the man fell backwards.

45

His full weight thudded into Dawlish, and he lost his balance.

In turn he hit a woman on the next step, and heard her scream in panic. As she tumbled, so those behind her fell. One after another the passengers on the staircase went down. The shouting and screaming increased with alarm and panic.

Dawlish was still falling, entangled in a bunch of crying, kicking, struggling people. Each time he tried to get to his feet someone or something tripped him up. Confused voices and orders sounded from above and below; then there followed the noise of breaking glass; after a moment the escalator stopped.

It jerked Dawlish downwards yet again, and for some seconds he could not steady himself enough to rise above knee level.

Someone hoisted him to his feet at last. With more willpower than strength, he staggered to a section of seats which had been cleared. A cup of tea was pushed into his hands.

'This'll cheer you up, mate,' said a vague voice. The cup rattled in the saucer, and the voice continued: 'Here—lemme hold it for you.'

It was then that Dawlish jerked his head back violently.

He had no actual reason for doing so; instinct more than anything else had warned him, instinct allied to the subconscious working of his mind. There was something amiss with the vague voice, with the quick arrival of the tea, something wrong in the fact that he was the first to be offered it. He did not reason it out as closely as that, but just jerked his head back. The hot tea spilled over his tunic.

'Steady, steady!' said the voice.

Dawlish shot up a hand, and gripped the wrist. It was a slim one, and the forearm was soft to his fingers. That helped him to understand why the voice had struck a false note; it had pretended to be a man's, actually it was a woman's.

'What's the marrer?' it asked, in sudden alarm. 'Lemme go!'

Dawlish tightened his grip, yet knew that he could not hold firmly enough. The cup fell as the woman who had brought the tea turned and ran into the gloom, pushing her way through the pressing crowd.

46

CHAPTER EIGHT

ADVENTURES OF A CUP

It was an hour before Dawlish was able to get away.

By then several dozen people who had been on the escalator had been treated for shock and minor injuries. The staircase was operating again, and one by one the sufferers had departed.

Dawlish had been singled out by the police for questioning, chiefly, he suspected, because the scene with the unknown woman had been noticed, and that when questioned he refused to give up the cup. He was deliberately vague in some of his answers, referring them to Chief Inspector Trivett.

Not until it was established that he had been at the head of the stairs, and therefore the first to fall, was he given permission to go home; then there was another argument about the cup, with the dregs of tea it contained. Dawlish did not want to explain his apparent affection for it, and was annoyed with himself for not arranging with the Y.M.C.A. attendant to buy it. He could have settled the argument easily enough; instead he had allowed it to become a major issue.

Trivett's name, and Dawlish's insistence on the matter being referred to him, finally won the day. Dawlish, smarting at his own clumsiness, eventually persuaded a porter to get him a taxi.

'Where to, sir?' asked the driver.

'88g Jermyn Street,' said Dawlish, 'and for the love of Mike go slowly.'

The cabby's eyes lighted on the carefully held cup, and touching his forehead he winked at the porter. Irritated, but aware that some explanation must be given, Dawlish put on an appropriate expression and said solemnly:

'Most important, driver. Mustn't spill the tea. Go very carefully indeed, understand? A wager. Five shillings extra for you if I get home without spilling it.'

'Very good, sir,' said the cabby cheerfully.

47

Dawlish climbed in carefully, holding the cup in front of him.

The cabby started slowly, and continued at a snail's pace, but despite his care the dregs in the cup lapped perilously near the top several times.

It was cold in the cab, and the wet patch where the tea had already spilt felt like ice. His teeth began to chatter, and he was at the limit of his forebearance when eventually the cab stopped and the driver, showing unusual consideration, jumped down from his seat and opened the door.

'All Sir Garnett, sir? Nothing spilled, I 'ope.'

'No, it's all right,' said Dawlish. He put a frozen hand to his breast pocket to get out his wallet, and then in the moonlight saw two figures approach.

'Pat!' exclaimed Felicity.

'What the devil have you got there?' demanded Trivett.

'Steady with it!' howled Dawlish as Trivett put out a hand for the cup. He paid the cabby, adding a generous tip.

'Fel, run me a hot bath, will you, I'm perished through. And I'll probably need a change of clothes.' He shivered again. Felicity said nothing but hurried upstairs, while more slowly Dawlish and Trivett walked in her wake.

'What *is* this?' demanded Trivett, a little acidly. 'You've kept us nearly two hours, drat you.'

'Only two?' asked Dawlish. 'I—Bill! Hold that cup in both hands, and don't spill a drop!'

Carefully they continued their way to the flat.

Carefully Trivett deposited the cup on a table.

'Well, we've got that safely,' said Dawlish with weary triumph. 'Bill, I want the stuff analysed as soon as can be.' He shivered, and Trivett hastily poured out a stiff peg of whisky. Dawlish took it from him, and by the time he was soaking in a hot bath much of his annoyance and self-reproach faded.

Felicity and Trivett held their patience admirably, until, warmed and fed, his clothes drying by the fire, he sat back in a voluminous dressing-gown and launched into his story.

Neither made any comment until he had finished, and then they started to speak together.

'But——' began Felicity.

48

'Who——' said Trivett.

Dawlish shrugged.

'I don't know who started the shindy, but I do think Simon J. Simon had something to do with it. I fell into the thing with my eyes wide open, I think that annoyed me more than anything else.'

'Why should Simon start it?' Felicity demanded.

Dawlish said thoughtfully : 'I thought he didn't notice me, but he must have done do, and being a careful man made all the necessary arrangements to be sure that I didn't get to his home ground. A large query hangs over Simon's head, I think.'

Trivett frowncd. 'Y'know, Pat, you can't possibly hang this on Simon. It could have been an accident.'

Dawlish stared at him. 'Is that the official police view?'

'Not necessarily. What I mean is, that you've got nothing definite against Simon.'

'Hmm,' said Dawlish. 'I thought that was what I had been telling you, I can't be in the best of form. No, we can't tie this on to Simon, but we do know that the gentleman wants watching.'

'But why *should* he do it?' Felicity insisted.

'Because he didn't like being followed,' said Dawlish.

'Then why visit you?' asked Trivett.

'I don't know all the answers, damn it.'

'No,' said Trivett, leaning back in his chair, 'but do you know any of them? The point is, Pat, you can't be sure that it's anything to do with Simon. Someone else might have been watching for you, followed you and tried to put this over.'

'Tried?' asked Dawlish. 'Whoever did it succeeded too darned well.' He hesitated for a moment, and then shrugged : 'All right, I'll grant that it could have been someone else. There's certainly nothing hard and fast against Simon, and the man might be quite genuine. You didn't take to him, did you?'

'No,' said Trivett frankly. 'But I don't like a lot of aliens, even when they're perfectly honest fellows.'

'Example of the police force being fair,' said Dawlish.

'Do we have to keep talking round the problem?' demanded Felicity. 'Or are you going to try to think?'

'Reproof from a lady,' murmured Dawlish. 'She's right, too,' He stubbed out his cigarette, and looked into the blazing coal fire. 'Actually, darling, I don't know that there's a lot we can talk about until we know more than we do now. I'm hoping you'll be able to help us there, Bill.'

Trivett said: 'I don't think I can. I've been telling Felicity that all I know is that Cranton arranged for us to give you whatever help you needed, and we sent word to the counties to do the same. What it was about, I don't know.'

'You knew Breddon's death would interest me,' countered Dawlish.

'Cranton told us that it concerned Wilson and Breddon,' said Trivett. 'I don't know anything more than that.'

'Does anyone?' Felicity asked.

There was a momentary silence. Felicity looked from one man to the other, seeing that what she had said had struck each of them in the same way. Dawlish's face was bleak, his eyes holding an expression which she knew well, and disliked. It told her that he was not thinking of her, nor of anything personal, that he was looking into the future and, perhaps, the past; and that he was facing a problem which had suddenly grown acute, developing proportions which he had not seen before.

He said at last: 'That's the question—does anyone know? The answer is that three people *did* know what it was about, and a fourth probably knows something. The fourth is Georgette Wilson; I hope to God she's still alive.'

Startled, Felicity said: 'What are you driving at?'

'The obvious, darling. Wilson knew, and presumably Breddon did; both are dead. Cranton knows, but he's pretty well sealed up for some days to come. Georgette remains—I hope. We've got to find her within twelve hours. What can you do about it, Bill?'

Trivett was on his feet, approaching the telephone.

'I'll get the call out. She was at Salisbury at what time?'

'Say half-past three,' said Dawlish. 'The Salisbury police should have been trying to find her, and I asked Fowler—the Super down there—to watch the Royal Hotel at Amesbury. It's probably in his district, or near enough to give him authority. Ted and the Blakes are keeping an eye open, too. If Georgette was persuaded to go away with the Mooneys——'

'Who're they?' Trivett demanded from the telephone.

'People not nice to know. I told you to try to locate them, remember?'

'Yes,' said Trivett, and then spoke into the telephone.

Dawlish heard him give instructions for a countrywide search to be made for Georgette Wilson. That done, he replaced the receiver and turned to Dawlish.

'We won't lose any more time than we can help, Pat. I didn't get them going on Simon. I'll get back to the Yard and learn what I can about the gentleman myself.'

He took his hat and coat, waved an airy goodbye and was gone. A lump of coal fell from the fire spraying red-hot cinders close to a rug.

Felicity swept them back. On her knees, she said suddenly:

'Pat, what do you really think of Simon?'

Dawlish hesitated, and then said quietly: 'I think Simon J. Simon came here to find out whether I'd had a talk with Cranton or not, and I think he decided that I had, and thought it time that I joined Wilson and Breddon in the happy hereafter. Not a comforting thought, but we can bear with it.'

Felicity said: 'I don't expect a lot of comfort until it's over. Do you know anything more?'

'Not a darned thing beyond what Georgette told us, and if she's right then it's connected with after-the-war problems, and plans for reconstruction. That doesn't really hold water. Cranton isn't a post-war man, he's engaged wholly on current problems. What's more, he wouldn't be the only man to be in the know at Whitehall. Someone else must have had partial facts.'

'I've no doubt you'll learn them in time,' said Felicity briskly.

'If some gentleman at the War Office doesn't decide I was called in by mistake,' Dawlish said grimly.

'What gave you that idea?'

'It just came.' He paused a minute and then went on jerkily: 'I wonder if Tim's learnt anything at Wilson's place?'

Felicity looked at him sharply, realising that the accident on the escalator had shaken him more than he would admit. She said firmly :

'Bed for you, my boy.'

'Confound it,' grumbled Dawlish, stifling a sneeze, 'how can I go to bed in the middle of this?' But after ten minutes wrangling he gave in.

Another violent fit of sneezing made him forget everything but the cold which was revealing itself all too thoroughly. Felicity dosed him with hot whisky, two hot-water bottles and three aspirins, and within twenty minutes he was asleep.

It was while Dawlish was sleeping that three men met in earnest conclave in a room in Whitehall.

A fourth was expected, no less a person than the Under-Secretary to whom Cranton had talked of Dawlish. The trio waited for half an hour for the missing member, and then went into conference. They did not know the full circumstances; only the Under-Secretary, Cranton, Wilson and Breddon had known those. One, a corpulent Brigadier nicknamed Boodles, remembered that Dawlish had made a particularly scathing remark in his presence; it had rankled. He saw no point in allowing Dawlish and other active-service officers to be re-tained from their units for a matter which could easily be handled through the normal channels. Knowing that Cranton was out of action, he immediately got into touch with Cran-ton's senior assistant.

At the end of an hour it was decided that Dawlish should go back to his unit.

On the following morning, Dawlish awakened more clear-headed. His voice was hoarse, but otherwise he felt well enough. He called to Felicity :

'Nothing from Tim or Ted, I suppose?'

'Nothing,' Felicity told him, any further remarks she was about to make being cut short by a ring at the front door.

'Tim for a fortune,' said Dawlish, and sipped the tea Felicity had brought him. Her face was expressionless when she returned, bearing a telegram. Dawlish scowled as he tore it open, and read the words he had been dreading :

Special work terminated. Return to your unit forthwith.

52

CHAPTER NINE

NOTHING TO DO?

'Well,' said Dawlish, 'that's it.'

'How bright you are, darling,' said Felicity.

'I don't think I can bear you in a funny mood just now,' declared Dawlish, waving the telegram to one side. He pushed the bedclothes back, and stared up at Felicity. 'Away, shameless one. Let me mourn in peace.'

He dressed slowly, his mood changing before he had finished. Felicity had set the small table for breakfast in the kitchen, and he was more than ready for it. Halfway through his second piece of toast and marmalade, he said placidly:

'Darling, I hate to shatter that mood of secret gladness you're trying to suppress, but if you think that I'm going back to manoeuvres, out of the way of Simon J., forget it.'

'But you can't stay away,' Felicity said quickly. 'You'll be called a deserter.'

'Not me,' said Dawlish. 'I'm going to the War Office to see Chumley, Under-Secretary for War. He's a man of sense, I hear.'

'You'll see a couple of clerks,' said Felicity grimly, 'and you'll come away in a worse temper than you were in last night.'

'Like to bet on it?' demanded Dawlish.

Felicity eyed him with motherly concern.

'Pat, your cold's affected your mind. Do you really think you can break into Chumley's room and get him to listen?'

She broke off, at a ring at the front door bell.

'Tim, I wonder?' she asked eagerly, and jumped to her feet.

This time, however, it was Trivett, who followed her into the kitchen, accepting the cup of coffee which Felicity held out to him.

'News, Pat,' he said. 'No sugar, thanks.'

Dawlish opened the envelope Trivett held towards him, and took out a slip of paper. On it were several lines in handwriting so bad that it was almost indecipherable. The word 'arsenic', however, was clear enough.

Dawlish actually beamed.

'Well, well, well, so the dregs in that cup of tea actually contained twenty-odd grains of arsenic, enough to kill even the charmed life of Patrick Dawlish! Things are certainly beginning to work!'

'You think so?'

'I'm sure of it. I'll wave this evidence in Chumley's face, and if he isn't convinced that it's really worth my while to go on, I'll give the War Office up for good.' Dawlish tucked the message into his pocket, and added: 'Anything else?'

'Nothing much.'

'How much is nothing much?'

'There's no report on anyone except Simon,' Trivett told him, 'and that's vague but satisfactory, as far as it goes. He's an economic expert, violently anti-Nazi, working with the full approval of the government.'

'Hm. I wish I could see the tie-up, Bill. War Office and Economics don't seem to go together. No word from Amesbury?'

'Only that the Mooneys fetched up there yesterday. Ted Beresford is still there, and so are your friends the Blakes.'

'Hmm. What is there from Wilson's home?'

'Nothing more at all. I've confirmed the statement that Wilson received threats to retire, or go on sick leave. All three of the secretaries read the letter he received yesterday, the one he took to Cranton.'

'Wrong,' said Dawlish. 'He took it to Breddon. Breddon sent him to the Colonel. Why, why, why?' he demanded helplessly.

Trivett finished his coffee while Felicity told him of the recall telegram. Trivett made little in the way of comment, but expressed doubt that Dawlish would be able to get it countermanded.

'That's right, look as pleased as Felicity about it,' grumbled Dawlish.

The two men went off together, but before Dawlish left Trivett at the end of Whitehall, he had arranged for a plain-clothes man to watch the flat. In no circumstances did he intend to leave Felicity alone and unguarded. Arriving at the War Office Dawlish was shown into the presence of a thin-faced, preternaturally solemn man who was a private secretary to Horatio Chumley, the Under-Secretary for War.

Dawlish had been elated at the comparative speed with which he reached this sanctum; but the sight of the solemn face and the tight lips checked him. This man was not one who could be approached genially; Dawlish decided that he must be side-tracked at all costs.

'I thought,' he said, 'that I was to see Mr. Chumley.'

'I am afraid that is quite impossible,' said the secretary promptly. 'He is engaged in conference.'

'I can wait,' said Dawlish. 'The matter is both urgent and important.'

The tight lips parted, something like a sigh escaped them before they closed again and the man said coldly:

'The Under-Secretary is at a conference out of London, Captain Dawlish, and I am in no position to say when he will return. I suggest that you write to him, and I will see that the letter is placed before him as soon as he can conveniently give attention to it.'

He did not add: 'Good morning,' although Dawlish would not have been surprised by the words of dismissal, but his manner was clear enough. Dawlish retained his seat, and even crossed his legs, rooting in his pockets for a cigarette.

'Did you know that his life is in danger?' he asked casually. He was lighting a match when the secretary said more sharply:

'I beg your pardon?'

Dawlish pushed his chair back and stood up. He said sharply:

'I'm telling you that the Under-Secretary's life is in acute danger, and unless I'm able to see him within the hour it will probably be too late. Where is he?'

The man wilted.

'But—but he is away, he went away last night. I—Captain Dawlish, are you aware of what you are saying?'

'I'm so aware of it that I know he'll be as dead as Breddon

55

and Wilson within the next few hours, unless you people move. Where is the Minister for War?'

He had created an impression all right. The secretary in turn pushed his chair back, and approached the door.

'I won't keep you long,' he said, and went out with the haste of a scared rabbit.

Dawlish smiled grimly, wondering whether he could support his statement with anything more than arguable theories, and decided that if Chumley, when he arrived, did not prove a more genial soul than the secretary there would be the devil to pay.

'Will you come this way, please, Captain Dawlish?'

Now for it, thought Dawlish.

The secretary led Dawlish into a vast room in which three women were typing furiously. There was a second, closed, door.

This the secretary tapped, and opened.

'Captain Dawlish, sir.' He stood aside for Dawlish to enter another vast room, this time occupied by a single man at a desk as large as a double bed.

Dawlish saw a shock of white hair above a youthful-looking face in which blue eyes of exceptional directness were shadowed by jutting black brows. They gave an oddly contradictory impression. The hair was an old man's, the face was that of a man in the prime of life, rather florid and clean-shaven, with a powerful chin and a large, bony nose.

In the twinkling of an eye which passed between his being announced and the sight of the man, Dawlish realised that his whole build-up had to be completely altered; this man was not Chumley, the Under-Secretary. He was the Rt. Hon. Gordon McKye, the Secretary for War.

McKye's voice was only faintly accented; forty years in London had robbed it of its Scottish intonation. A man of intellectual power, one of the rebels against the pre-war and pre-Norwegian Government, he had made a thoroughly good job of his post at the War Office, although it was rumoured that even he was constantly frustrated by a policy which had taken a long time to key itself up to total war demands.

He waved towards a chair.

'Sit down, Dawlish.' He pushed cigarettes across the vast desk, and took a lighter from his pocket. He waited until Dawlish was smoking, and then went on: 'Now what's the trouble?'

Dawlish decided that the wise course would be complete frankness, and took the crumpled telegram from his pocket.

'That began it, sir.'

McKye glanced down at the recall.

'Hmm. What special work had you been called on?'

'I was to meet Colonel Cranton in Salisbury,' Dawlish said, 'and the meeting was prevented. You've probably heard of that.' McKye nodded, and Dawlish went on: 'I had nothing very much to work on, but there were some odds and ends. I'd asked for help, and two of my friends were released for the duration of the emergency, whatever it is. They're both working; their recall at this juncture might be fatal.'

McKye raised an eyebrow expressively.

'Fatal to what, Dawlish?'

'The successful culmination of the investigation,' said Dawlish amiably. 'I don't know what Cranton wanted; I do know that it concerned Professor Wilson and Lord Breddon. Both have been killed. An attempt was made to kill me, after I had deliberately created the impression that I knew what was on foot. I inferred that Mr. Chumley gave Colonel Cranton instructions: and from that inferred an acute danger to Mr. Chumley's life.'

'I see,' said McKye. He spoke with composure. 'You're not satisfied with the matter being handled by the normal channels?'

'I'm satisfied that Colonal Cranton didn't think it could be, sir, and he isn't a man to act without reason. There are a dozen things that need doing, and no time should be lost. Presuming,' Dawlish added quietly, 'that the murder of Professor Wilson and Lord Breddon are considered of outstanding importance, sir.'

He thought that McKye's eyes twinkled.

'Yes, you can presume that,' said the War Minister. 'All right, Dawlish, I'll see that this is countermanded. I was told what to expect from you,' he added, and Dawlish wondered whether this seemingly innocent sentence held a barb.

'If they've been sent to Captains Jeremy and Beresford——' he began, only for McKye to say:

'I'll look after all of it, Dawlish. Now—do you *seriously* think there is danger for Chumley?'

'Yes,' Dawlish said crisply. 'Everyone who knows what Wilson was working on has been attacked. The evidence is that an effort is being made to cancel it right out.' He paused. 'Do you know what it is, sir?'

McKye's eyebrows went up again.

'Up to a point, yes. I don't know everything. I was to have seen Chumley about it this morning, but he hasn't turned up yet.' McKye paused, and then went on slowly: 'You've no definite reason for thinking that he might have been attacked?' Dawlish said: 'I thought it probable. How late is he?'

'About two hours,' said McKye.

'Hmm. That doesn't sound too good. Will you tell me the general outlines, sir? I'm working in the dark, and it isn't helpful.'

'No, I suppose not,' said McKye drily. 'Yes, Dawlish, I can tell you. Cranton would have done so had things been normal. Professor Wilson and Lord Breddon were on the Committee for the Restoration and Improvement of Economic Relationship in the Post-War Period. You'd know that. The work implied investigations into certain economic procedures before and during the war, and I understand that Professor Wilson brought some facts to light which react strongly on the present problems. Do you follow?'

'I'm trying to see the connection between this and the War Office,' said Dawlish frankly.

'At the moment I can't tell you that,' said McKye frankly. 'There is a connection, but not so clear-cut as you imagine. The matter affects the Home Office equally, perhaps even more so, and in any case comes to us through the Ministry for Economic Warfare. I'm not going to believe that you need to know the details, Dawlish, but I can tell you that there is a body of men working against the interests of the country, and that body has undoubtedly been instrumental in killing Wilson. I think myself that they killed Breddon, but there is no real evidence of that yet. I think that all Cranton could have told you was that this body or organisation existed; Wilson would have gone into closer detail with you. Does that help?'

Dawlish shrugged. 'It has to, sir.'

'I'm glad you see it like that,' said McKye. 'I wish——'

He stopped abruptly, for the telephone bell rang. He lifted the receiver.

Dawlish saw McKye's hand tighten, heard his exclamation. He heard McKye say 'Hold on,' and then:

'Chumley's dead,' he said flatly. 'His valet has just found him in his room.'

CHAPTER TEN

THE TRAIL OF GEORGETTE

Dawlish said afterwards that two things followed the murder of Chumley. He was given what amounted to a *carte blanche* on the case; and he found himself no longer groping for odds and ends which might help him to decide what it was about. That was because it forced him to concentrate on Georgette Wilson, and others connected with her.

Half an hour after leaving the War Office he was in the flat in Chelsea which Chumley, a middle-aged bachelor, had used for many years. The police had not arrived, for Chumley's valet had had the good sense to get in touch immediately with the War Office.

The flat was one of four, and Dawlish learned quickly that the other three had been empty for some time. The valet, who proved to be Chumley's only servant, was an oldish man with a lined face. He was in an acute stage of emotion.

Chumley had been found in bed slumped down on his pillows. In his right hand had been a slip of paper.

Dawlish turned to Riddle.

'You've touched nothing?'

'No.' The word was barely audible.

'Did he have any visitors last night?' Dawlish was looking at a coffee cup on a table next to the bed.

'No.'

'Do you mean he didn't have visitors, or that you weren't aware of any?'

'I—retired early.' Riddle gulped.

'Who made his coffee, or whatever it was?'

'He—made it—himself,' Riddle said. 'He did so—frequently. Always'—there was a long pause, and then thickly—'most considerate in every way.'

'What time did you see him last?'

'About—eleven o'clock.'

Dawlish looked about the room. There was ample evidence that Chumley was a man of tidy habits; his clothes were neatly folded, and some papers were placed in an orderly pile next to the cup and saucer; the top one was marked: *Secret*. A cigarette, half-burned, rested on an otherwise clean ashtray.

Dawlish said quietly: 'Did he smoke much?'

'A—a great deal, sir.'

'So there was another ashtray,' said Dawlish.

'It—it is likely, sir. He may have placed it in the kitchen, or in his study.'

'See if that's where it is, will you?' asked Dawlish, and as the servant went out Dawlish prised the paper very gently from Chumley's fingers. There was nothing to indicate that it had anything to do with the man's death, but there was the possibility that it could be connected. He glanced at the signature, since there was no address at the top of the letter, and stiffened in surprise.

It read:

Dear Mr. Chumley,

Thank you for your invitation. There is nothing I can usefully do, I am afraid. I expect to be away indefinitely.

Yours very truly,
Georgette Wilson.

Dawlish tightened his lips as he read the note again. He

heard Riddle walking towards the front door, and a moment moment later, Trivett's voice. The Inspector entered briskly, bringing with him a thick set, grey haired man whom Dawlish recognised as Dr. Lees-Gretton, the Divisional police surgeon. A gruff man at all times, Lees-Gretton nodded curtly and bent over Chumley's body.

'Have you found anything?' Trivett asked.

'Nothing yet,' said Dawlish. 'Let's leave the doctor to it, and go and see Riddle.'

They found the valet in the study, a large room handsomely furnished with an eye to bachelor comfort.

'Any luck?' Dawlish asked.

'The other ashtray, sir. It has been emptied into this waste-paper basket.'

Dawlish picked up the previous day's evening paper, lying on a chair, and very carefully emptied the basket on to it. He examined the shapeless stubs while Trivett watched him curiously.

Dawlish said: 'Riddle, you're sure that you heard no one else here last night?'

'Positive, sir.'

'You would have known had anyone else come before, say, midnight?'

'I could not be sure of anything after eleven-thirty, sir.'

'Fair enough,' said Dawlish. 'All right, thanks. We'll need you again in a few minutes, I expect.'

As Riddle went out, closing the door, Dawlish turned to Trivett.

'I hope he's not lying, but I think Chumley did have a visitor. There are some corked-tip cigarettes, and on one a small smudge of lipstick. Plenty of work for your hearties there, I imagine. I wonder if——' He paused, and then went on: 'I wonder if it could have been Georgette? Apparently he sent a message to her, asking her to see him. She regretted that she couldn't in a polite little note that I didn't expect.'

'Why should you expect anything?' Trivett demanded.

'My dear Bill!' exclaimed Dawlish. 'We'll all be expecting something to the end of time!' He rubbed his nose, and then added more reasonably: 'Chumley had the note in his hand when he died. I assumed from that that he received it sometime yesterday. If she wrote it, then she did so after leaving Salisbury yesterday, which brings us to sometime last evening. She certainly wasn't cool and collected when we last saw her, but the note was perfectly natural. Either she recovered quickly, or someone else wrote it for her.'

'You're going ahead a bit, aren't you?' Trivett objected. 'Anyone could force themselves to write a short note without letting his or her feelings show in it.'

Dawlish raised an eyebrow.

'If you'd seen Georgette yesterday afternoon you wouldn't be so sure. What's worrying me,' he added abruptly, 'is the possibility that, in spite of her note, she did in fact come to see him. These small cigarettes, the lipstick——'

'You've no reason at all for thinking she's been here,' said Trivett dogmatically.

'All right, call it a hunch,' said Dawlish. 'Anyhow, he had a woman visitor last night, or sometime yesterday, and she smoked small cigarettes, some of the ends of which were in the ashtray that Chumley emptied before he went into the bedroom. I wonder when Riddle last cleaned the thing?'

He stepped through to the hall, finding Riddle standing there indeterminately. Footsteps were echoing outside, and a shadow showed against the frosted glass panel of the front door.

'Keep them waiting a moment,' Dawlish said as the bell rang. 'What time did Mr. Chumley go into his study?'

'About ten o'clock, sir.'

'Was the ashtray empty then?'

'Yes, sir.'

'There can't be any doubt about that?'

'None at all,' Riddle assured him. 'I emptied it myself yesterday morning, and no one was in the study until the evening. I'm *quite* sure, sir.'

He moved towards the front door, and opened it.

On the threshold was Detective Sergeant Munk, a slow-moving, wide-shouldered man, with a permanent expression of aggressive pessimism. There were two other plainclothes men with him, and Dawlish knew that the routine work would be carried out not only well but expeditiously.

Before Munk and his men started their flashlight photography and fingerprint quest, the police surgeon joined Trivett and Dawlish. There was no evidence of foul play, he said, death was in all probability due to cerebral haemorrhage. Yes, it was just possible that it had been induced, but if so Dr. Lees-Gretton did not know that there was any way in which it could be proved. He gave an impression that he was too busy to stand and argue the point with Dawlish and Trivett.

'We'd better get Cartwright's opinion as soon as possible,' Dawlish mused. 'Thing is, was Chumley murdered as I think Breddon was.'

'Cartwright's opinion of him was cerebral haemorrhage induced by an overdose of adrenalin on a subject with a tendency towards heart weakness,' Trivett murmured. 'If Chumley had the same trouble, Cartwright will probably give the same opinion.'

'Hmm. Could mean that whoever gave them the stuff knew where their weakness lay. Interesting.'

'Aren't you getting away from the point?' asked Trivett.

'Point, what point? Oh yes——' Dawlish grinned. 'If Chumley was murdered, who killed him? Was it his woman visitor, who came here *after* Riddle had gone to bed, always assuming Riddle isn't lying? And was his woman visitor Georgette Wilson, who had declined an earlier invitation?'

'Well, I haven't got second sight,' said Trivett testily.

'You're in an obstructive mood,' Dawlish assured him. 'As a policeman, you wouldn't have Georgette's fingerprints by you, would you?'

'No,' said Trivett, 'but I'll tell you what I have got. They came in this afternoon. The police at Amesbury managed to get prints from the Mooneys.'

Dawlish said warmly: 'Nice work! We seem to have come a long way from Salisbury. It might even be too far. I wish,' he added, 'that I had heard from Ted and Tim. Why Tim's disappeared I just don't know. He was to find out what he could at Portiman Square, about the Professor's secretaries and Georgette. Well——' He spoke more briskly. 'We'd better have a look about the flat in earnest.'

Except for the papers which Chumley had by his bedside they found nothing of interest. The safe contained a couple of hundred pounds and some oddments of jewellery. Riddle said that they were family pieces, and that his employer had not been in the habit of receiving lady visitors. Now and again ladies from his constituency had visited the flat, but rarely alone. The valet adhered to his statement that he had been to bed by eleven o'clock, and that, to his knowledge, no one had visited the flat on that evening.

'Puzzling show,' Dawlish said when he left the flat with Trivett. 'Mysterious lady visitor to abode of confirmed and irreproachable bachelor. Letter from Georgette inferring that the confirmed bachelor had asked her to see him. Question—why?'

Trivett said: 'Aren't you losing sight of the fact that Chumley, Breddon and Wilson are all dead, Pat, and Cranton pretty close to it? All important members of the government, or government committees.'

'Do I look as if I'm forgetting it?' Dawlish asked gloomily.

'Well, yes, you do rather,' said Trivett, stepping into the police car. 'You seem to be concentrating on the girl's visit, and if it's a fact and not just a fancy, Chumley probably asked for it because he wanted to find out what she knew about her dead father's business. Obviously Wilson found something pretty big, to make Cranton get as busy as he did, and because of its size Cranton was able to move the War Office to really quick action. You've pointed out yourself that the only people who might know that Wilson knew are dead, or precious close to it.'

'He takes the words out of my mouth,' said Dawlish admiringly.

'Don't be a dolt,' said Trivett sharply. 'You're taking the line that Chumley's lady visitor, if any, is the main factor. I'm questioning it.'

'I think she's *really* important if she was Georgette,' amended Dawlish. 'Even if she wasn't, she might have drugged Chumley's night-cap. Wouldn't you call that important?'

'Only when, and if, we find that he *was* poisoned,' said Trivett a little stiffly.

'Yes, of course,' said Dawlish. 'First establish your facts, then explain them. Only there isn't time, I'll have to leave that to the police, Bill.'

'You're an irritating beggar in this mood,' declared Trivett. 'Can I give you a lift?'

'As far as Parliament Square will do fine; then you can do the rest of the journey in peace.'

Twenty minutes later Dawlish stood on the pavement of Parliament Square, watching Trivett drive away towards Scotland Yard. He stood motionless for some minutes after the car had disappeared, lost in thought. He heard Big Ben chime the quarter-past one.

Startled, he telephoned Felicity, who told him that no one else had called, and that nothing had happened—and would he be in for lunch?

'I don't think so, darling,' said Dawlish. 'Don't wait any longer, tuck into whatever you've prepared.'

'Thank you for your kind permission,' said Felicity drily. 'What happened?'

'Happened?' repeated Dawlish. 'Where?'

He heard Felicity draw in a deep breath, and smiled as he heard her tell him, more comprehensively than Trivett had done, that in certain moods he was unbearable. He waited until Felicity had exhausted her annoyance, and then apologised humbly, adding:

'Honestly, sweet, I'd forgotten what I left the flat for. Yes, everything's all right, and I've full marching orders. I'll be in for tea, so look pretty for me.'

He rang off, and walked slowly towards the Admiralty Arch, then on into the Mall. He was contemplating the wisdom of calling at the Aliens' Club and asking to see Simon J. Simon, and the idea grew on him. The club, a comparatively small one, was of considerable repute; no distinguished alien in Great Britain failed to join, and all alien visitors who were friendly towards this country were made honorary members for the duration of their stay.

Dawlish, entering the large doorway, was approached by a small, olive-skinned porter.

'Good morning, sir.'

'Good morning,' said Dawlish. 'Is Mr. Simon here, do you know?'

'I will find out, sir, in one moment.' The man stepped into his office, and lifted a telephone. A jabber of words followed, and then the telephone went down.

'Yes, sir, he is lunching in the Visitors' Room. Shall I send word to him, sir?'

'No, thanks,' said Dawlish. 'I'll go up.'

He was not long in finding the room. Entering unobtrusively he found that by standing near a screen he could see every corner of the room without the risk of being noticed by more than the few people nearest him.

He spotted Simon fairly quickly, and then caught his breath in astonishment.

The woman facing him, talking with every appearance of animation, was Georgette Wilson.

Dawlish's heart beat a shade faster as he watched the girl.

At Simon's table was another, younger man. Dawlish was irritated because he could not see the latter clearly, but the name of Gerald North sprang to his mind. Dawlish stood there for some seconds, undecided.

'A note for you, sir.'

Surprised, Dawlish felt a note slipped into his hand by a passing waiter.

Had Simon J. Simon anticipated his visit? With some excitement Dawlish unfolded the missive.

He read:

> What-ho, old son. Has she led me a dance! Don't queer my pitch, blast you—Tim.

Dawlish chuckled silently, and turned away. He retraced his footsteps, deep in thought. As he reached the head of the stairs a plump man hurried past him. A little surprised at such seemingly pointless energy Dawlish watched him disappear round a corner in the passage, and then forgot him.

'Excuse me, sir.'

Dawlish half-turned as a voice spoke to his right. He had

not noticed the door there open, and did not recognise the tall man who addressed him.

'Yes?'

'Are you Captain Dawlish, sir?'

'That's right,' said Dawlish, and wondered again whether Simon had seen him. How else could he be known at the club, for Tim would not have talked.

'There is a telephone message for you, sir,' said the attendant smoothly, and held the door open for Dawlish to step through.

Dawlish went unhesitatingly, and tripped over a foot which was pushed out in front of him. As he fell he caught a glimpse of the plump man with an arm upraised; and then he felt the sickening thud of a heavy weapon on the back of his head.

He was unconscious when he hit the ground.

CHAPTER ELEVEN

ALL FRIENDS TOGETHER

He had no idea how long he remained unconscious.

He came round slowly with an aching head, surprised to find he had suffered nothing worse. He saw that he was lying on a comfortable settee in a small, well-appointed room.

Gingerly he touched the back of his head.

It was tender, and there was a lump of some consequence. He remembered what had happened without rage or self-reproach, not doubting that even had he failed to accept the bait of the telephone call, some other way of trapping him would have been found before he left the club.

On the whole, he was well-satisfied. Undoubtedly some of the staff, and presumably some of the club's members, were involved, and that was a discovery of first importance.

A little shakily he stood up and approached the door; it was locked on the outside, which did not surprise him.

'A sandbag,' he murmured aloud, running a hand once again over the back of his head. 'They did it thoroughly, but they didn't want me seriously hurt. I wonder why?' He walked to the windows, finding that behind the heavy curtains they were boarded up to prevent blast. No chance, then, of him attracting attention that way. He resigned himself to waiting, glancing at his watch and finding that it was nearly half-past two.

His third cigarette was half-smoked when the door opened abruptly.

It was the plump man who entered, and Dawlish saw with some surprise that he was a Japanese.

The man closed the door behind him, turned the key in the lock, and then slid the key into his pocket. He advanced slowly.

'Captain Dawlish, I am delighted to make your acquaintance.'

'Really? You will forgive me if I do not reciprocate that delight,' said Dawlish coldly.

Precise and humourless the man ploughed on.

'Doubtless, Captain, you will be curious as to why it was considered necessary to take these unusual steps to ensure this interview. Yes?'

'Not really,' Dawlish told him casually.

'No?' The plump face expressed puzzlement. The man bowed. 'My name, please, is Oroshu, Kori Oroshu, at your service, Captain Dawlish.'

'How do you do,' said Dawlish politely.

'Thank you, I am well. I——'

'Supposing we cut the cackle?' Dawlish suggested. 'What do you want?'

Oroshu said: 'I have heard that you are an unusual man, Captain. It is not always wise to believe what one hears, but in this case——' His smile came again, brief, automatic and meaningless. 'I must explain my motive. It came to my ears that you were in considerable danger, that you might even be killed. You were in the club, of which I have the honour to be the manager.' Another bow. 'It was considered wise and kind to retain you here until the danger was past.'

68

'Oh?' said Dawlish woodenly.

'I am fully aware that it is difficult to believe,' went on Oroshu, 'but there are times when it is sensible to act first and to explain afterwards. So I decided. And at the same time, Captain, I can extend my apologies and also offer a word of advice which you may or may not accept, as you think fit.'

Dawlish looked down at the expressionless eyes. He did not trust them, nor the quick smile. He was practically convinced that the other was lying at high pressure. On the other hand, he felt bewilderment that Oroshu should choose to lie as he was doing; there must be a motive for it.

'My apologies then, my dear Captain. And my advice—you are in great danger, how great you are probably not aware. Many things of which you are ignorant are happening, and'— Oroshu shrugged—'there are people who think it might be wiser that way. I put it to you as a suggestion, Captain Dawlish. Knowledge can be dangerous, and the thirst for knowledge even more dangerous.'

Dawlish said: 'It had occurred to me, yes. How do you know that danger threatens, Oroshu?'

'There are ways of learning,' Oroshu said, earnestly, 'and there is danger in passing on information about those ways. It is my great hope, Captain, that you will be advised, and ask no questions. Your life was in acute danger this afternoon. Had you left the doors of this club you would have been killed. What I know I can say, how I learned is a different matter. There were three men waiting opposite the club, two with automatic rifles. They were seen, their objective was discovered, they were kept waiting, and now they have been advised that you have gone another way.' A quick, cunning smile. 'Had we told you this danger threatened, you would have insisted on going out. No warnings would have deterred you. I should not like to feel that I had allowed your death, Captain Dawlish. You understand?'

'No,' said Dawlish.

Oroshu shrugged. 'Too well I know that it is asking much of you, but those are the circumstances, those are the reasons for my attack on you. At your pleasure you can lodge a report to the police, who will doubtless cancel my permit to live comfortably and happily in this country which has always been my friend, but with which my country is at war. It is in your hands, Captain. This discussion was necessary, I took all steps to ensure it. The rest remains with you.'

Oroshu took the key from his pocket, and unlocked the door. Pulling it open he stood aside for Dawlish to pass.

'It is my earnest desire,' said Oroshu firmly, 'that you will allow me to show you to the side door. It will be wise to use that, I think.'

He led the way, finally standing aside with a low bow. Dawlish stepped into a narrow alleyway, to the left of which he saw the trees of St. James's Park. The door closed behind him, a little too quickly. He was alone, and comparatively unhurt.

'Well, well, well!' exclaimed Dawlish aloud. 'This is a new one on me.' He hesitated, and turned towards the Park.

No one appeared to take the slightest interest in him. He stepped across the road, glancing sharply at the grass behind the railings immediately in front of the Aliens' Club. The flattened surface and fresh cigarette ends were ample evidence that two or three men had been standing there.

He walked back to Trafalgar Square, inclined to congratulate himself on being alive. In the split second of consciousness before Oroshu had shanghaied him he had seen the possibility of being killed before he went further in the affair, had believed that he was trapped by as simple a bait as had ever been used.

Yet here he was, quite free.

He walked briskly towards Jermyn Street, hurrying up the stairs of 88g. Felicity's expression sobered him. He put an arm about her waist.

'Trouble?' he asked.

Felicity said, tight-lipped: 'Tim's just come in.'

Dawlish went into the lounge.

Tim Jeremy was lying on the settee, his head resting against blood-stained pillows. His tunic, too, was stained with blood, his face a deathly white.

Dawlish snapped: 'Did he say anything?'

'He whispered "Georgette",' Felicity said, 'and then collapsed. He——'

She did not need to go on. Dawlish went down on one knee, the better to examine the injured head.

'Have you sent for a doctor?'

'I rang Miller, but he was engaged.'

'I'll try him again,' Dawlish said tersely.

This time a man's decisive voice answered. Dawlish knew Dr. Miller well, and had no difficulty in getting him to come at once to the flat. Satisfied with that promise, Dawlish returned to help Felicity, but there was little more that he could do.

Tim Jeremy remained unconscious, and Dawlish said low-voiced:

'So he had Georgette on his mind. He was lunching at the Aliens' Club with an unknown lovely, Georgette was with Simon and another man; North, I fancy. Has anything else turned up?'

'Ted rang through to say that nothing's happened down there,' said Felicity. 'I told him you'd ring him. He's at an inn near the Royal. Freddie and Hermina are still at the Royal, with the Mooneys.'

Dawlish grunted. He was on edge until Miller arrived. A short, dark man, consultant physician to several of the larger London hospitals, he made a quick examination and then straightened up.

'He'll be all right,' he said, 'but I'd like him taken to a nursing-home.'

Dawlish nodded agreement.

'I'll have an ambulance round in an hour,' promised Miller. He gave a quick smile, and clapped Dawlish on the shoulder as he made for the door. 'You're at it again, I gather.'

Dawlish grinned non-committally as he saw the doctor out, and then returned to Felicity. He could see she had been badly shaken, and decided that for the time being it would be wiser to say nothing about his own misadventure.

'Supposing I make a cup of tea?' he suggested. 'And I could do with something to eat, too.' He linked an arm through hers and they went into the kitchen. Felicity put on a kettle, and Dawlish rummaged in the larder. As they prepared a snack, Felicity said hopelessly:

'Is it ever going to straighten out, Pat? It's just one series of disconnected incidents after another.'

'They'll link in time,' said Dawlish comfortably. 'Georgette and Wilson's secretaries are the people to concentrate on.' He went on to describe what had happened at the War Office, telling the story in such a way as to make Felicity laugh.

The ambulance arrived soon afterwards.

Dawlish assured himself of the driver's credentials, and those of the attendant, and then watched Tim being put on a stretcher. The nursing home that Miller had recommended was only five minutes walk from Jermyn Street, and Dawlish hoped that before the day was out Tim would be able to talk.

As the ambulance drove out of sight, the telephone rang.

Dawlish picked up the receiver not knowing quite what to expect. He was relieved to hear Trivett's voice.

Briefly Dawlish told him what had happened, ending:

'The only person on Tim's mind as far as we know was Georgette Wilson, Bill. It's beginning to work my way—or don't you think so?'

Trivett said: 'Yes, Pat. I know so, now. We've had reports in from the inquiries made about last night—Chumley's flat, I mean. Georgette was there. She arrived about midnight, and left soon after one o'clock. We've just had a further report that she's now at 31 Portiman Square, with North, the secretary. Do you want to go along?'

CHAPTER TWELVE

PORTIMAN SQUARE

'Yes,' said Dawlish. 'I want to go along, Bill. The question is, do you?'

Trivett's answering murmur over the wire could have been taken in a number of ways. Dawlish grinned, as he went on:

'There's a lot to be said for leaving it to me for the time being, but if you can't do that you can at least let me go along to see the lady for half an hour before you weigh in.'

Trivett said a trifle drily that he'd had instructions to leave it to Dawlish. He made no comment on what he thought of the instructions, although Dawlish imagined that the policeman, and the Yard at large, would not be pleased. For his own part, his heart leapt; McKye had doubtless arranged things with the Home Office. His main concern was, of course, to get results without working too much through the police, and thus getting the Press on the scene.

'Well, that's thoughtful of someone,' Dawlish said. 'You're having the place watched, of course?'

'We certainly are,' said Trivett emphatically.

'That sounds as if you're employing an army.'

'I'm leaving the army to you,' said Trivett acidly. 'Actually, Pat, if it were anyone but you I would be damned annoyed about it. As it is, I've got the house surrounded in case of accident, and I'll be near at hand.'

'Why the cordon?' asked Dawlish.

'Because a surprising number of men have gone into the house today,' Trivett told him. 'In ones and twos, but probably twenty-five altogether—I haven't the latest figure by me. Just why they've gone I don't know. They may be strong-arm gents, and I don't propose to take chances.' Trivett paused. 'How long shall I give you inside?'

'Make it an hour,' decided Dawlish. 'Well, goodbye, old son, and don't get too annoyed with upstart amateurs.'

He rang off on Trivett's grunt, then turned to explain things to Felicity. Both were surprised that arrangements had been made for the police to hold their hand until Dawlish had paid a visit. Dawlish was by no means sure that it was the compliment he might like to imagine, and Felicity said worriedly:

'Right from the start there's been something we don't understand, darling, and it's getting on my nerves. I'd like to come along with you.'

'Leave that to next time,' said Dawlish uneasily. 'I may have to get away in a hurry, and you won't want to make complications. I wish,' he added, 'that there was someone here with you.'

'Well, there's a policeman outside,' said Felicity staunchly, 'what more can a girl want!'

Dawlish left Jermyn Street at a quarter to four, unsettled in mind because of the persistence of the unusual. There were so many loose ends! He shrugged gloom aside, however, took a taxi to the end of Portiman Square, and then walked along to Number 31.

He saw two or three plain-clothes men, and had he not known what Trivett had told him he would have thought there was a suspiciously large number of taxi-drivers about.

A light wind rustled through the trees and shrubbery which centred the Square. The iron railings had been removed, giving it an unfinished appearance. Dawlish found Number 31 near a road which led to Oxford Street.

Three private cars and two taxis were outside.

Twenty-five visitors, Trivett had said; surely that was unusual? Dawlish saw that it might be because Wilson had died, and then remembered that he had not seen any report of the Professor's death in the paper. He thought again of the report in the *Courier*, which had anticipated Wilson's intention to take a rest in the country.

North had arranged for that to be published; did he know that Wilson was being threatened before the disclosure which Georgette had forced?

Dawlish rang the bell, waited for thirty seconds or more, and then rang again. He heard footsteps approaching, and confused voices.

A youthful-looking man opened the door.

Dawlish did not have time to take much stock of him, but had an impression of an honest and pleasant countenance. Then an older man came quickly to the door, saying:

'I'm sorry I was detained, sir.'

The younger man turned away, going into a room on the right of the hall. Dawlish held out his card.

'Miss Wilson, please,' he said.

'I'm afraid, sir——' the oldish man began.

'I know she's in, and I must see her,' said Dawlish sharply. The servant's face showed uncertainty and some degree of confusion. Dawlish's own uncompromising expression apparently decided him. He bowed and went off hurriedly.

Dawlish looked about him.

There was evidence of wealth and good taste in the hall. A finely-carved oak settle ran along one wall, and immediately above it hung a few early prints of old London. A Persian carpet of some value covered the floor.

The wait was a long one.

After five minutes Dawlish was about to step towards the room where the old man had entered when the door opposite it opened and the youthful-looking man he had first seen came towards him.

'Good afternoon, Captain Dawlish. My name is North, one of the late Professor Wilson's secretaries. I'm afraid it's impossible for you to see Miss Wilson this afternoon.'

'I don't think so,' Dawlish said quietly.

North frowned.

'Miss Wilson is seeing no one, except by appointment.'

Dawlish smiled amiably.

'Has she seen my card?'

'I don't really see that it concerns you,' snapped North, on the verge of losing his temper. 'If you care to make an appointment for tomorrow——'

Dawlish said: 'I intend seeing Miss Wilson within the next five minutes, or I shall obtain a warrant to search the house until I find her. And I can assure you that once the police start with search warrants it's hard to say where the show will stop.'

'What the devil are you talking about?' snapped North.

'You'll learn,' said Dawlish. 'Which room is she in?'

'She's not——'

Dawlish realised he was getting nowhere. North's purpose was to prevent a meeting, and nothing short of physical violence would make him change his mind. Time, for Dawlish, was the chief factor. Unless he showed up within an hour, Trivett would act.

He clenched his right hand, and before North knew what was coming brought his fist up in a blow which took the man squarely beneath the chin. North staggered back, but before he could fall, Dawlish had hold of him.

Quickly looking round the hall, Dawlish's eye lighted on the settle. He lifted the seat and saw with a sigh of relief there was space enough for North's body, and gaps round the hinges to ensure that he would not die of suffocation.

He bundled him in, and then walked towards the room into which North had gone earlier. It was, presumably, a drawing-room; but there was no one in it. Another door led from it into the next room. This, too, was empty.

Dawlish frowned, returned to the hall, and tried the room where the servant had gone. It led to a dining-room with a service door to the domestic quarters.

'How many *more* rooms?' Dawlish murmured, and went cautiously through the service doorway.

A narrow passage led to a butler's pantry which in turn took him into the kitchen itself. Smoke from a cigarette curled up from an ashtray.

'I don't like it,' Dawlish murmured. 'I don't like it at all.' He returned to the hall, hesitated, then went to the porch. He saw a taxi on the far side of the road; Trivett was talking to its driver.

Dawlish raised a hand.

Trivett approached promptly, and Dawlish said in a whisper: 'They're either all upstairs, or it's a trick. Are the houses on either side being watched?'

'No one will get out of here unless we want them to,' Trivett assured him. 'What's happened?'

'Nothing of importance yet,' Dawlish said. 'Come with me, will you?'

'I'll have a word with Munk, first,' said Trivett.

Alone, Dawlish turned to the settle and lifted the lid. North's eyes glared at him. Silently Dawlish helped him out, wondering how to explain the man's plight to Trivett.

A voice said sharply: 'Put your hands up, Captain Dawlish.'

Dawlish stood motionless. He did not know whether one man or more were behind him. He did know that there was menace in the thin voice which repeated waspishly:

'Put your hands up!'

In one rapid movement Dawlish had turned and faced the

man and fired.

At the same time a bullet from the thin-voiced man's gun buried itself in the wall. Dawlish's bullet, however, had found its mark in the man's shoulder.

He staggered, and then pitched forward on his face. Footsteps sounded from outside; Trivett came in, running.

Dawlish said: 'Someone was about, Bill. We'd better get the others in.' He gripped North's elbow. 'Where's Georgette? My God, if you don't answer I'll crack your ruddy jaw! Where is she?'

North's voice, when it came, was dazed and uncertain.

'She was upstairs. I don't know who—that—is.' He was staring towards the wounded man, and Dawlish could see that the attack, followed by the sight and sound of the shooting, had unnerved the secretary. Yet it was surprising to find North trying to establish innocence—or ignorance—at that juncture.

'How many others are there?' Dawlish snapped.

'No one.'

Impatiently Dawlish stepped towards the stairs, as Trivett came in at the head of a small bunch of men. He started up the stairs three at a time, reached the first landing, and then heard a shout from above.

'Keep back, keep back!'

Instinctively he stopped, peering upwards.

He saw a man kneeling behind an overturned chair, and the nose of a tommy-gun.

He saw a pair of slanting, Oriental eyes which reminded him strangely of Oroshu. Lifting his revolver he fired. The bullet struck the tommy-gun as he had hoped it would do. The stream of bullets which came from it spattered the wall. Before the man who was firing it could regain control, Dawlish had fired again; the man dropped backwards with a bullet wound in his head.

Dawlish scrambled over the upturned chair. He could hear movement from above and high-pitched voices speaking in a non-European tongue.

Japs, he thought. Japs, of course!

Trivett reached his side, breathing heavily.

'Where are they? Which door?'

'We'll learn,' said Dawlish. 'I want that girl, damn the rest of them.' He tried the handle of the first door he came to. It opened, but the bedroom beyond was empty. The second door opened as easily. He saw a four-poster bed. There was someone lying on it. He went nearer, and saw that it was Georgette Wilson.

But there was something dreadfully wrong.

He reached her in three strides, and saw a noose about her neck, drawn very tight; it was attached to one of the posts of the bed. He could not be sure whether she was breathing as he took a penknife from his pocket and cut first the cord then eased it away from the girl's neck.

He took her wrist, and was feeling for her pulse when Trivett entered.

'What the——' began Trivett.

'I'll look after her,' said Dawlish tersely. 'You carry on.'

He discerned a faint movement of Georgette's pulse, and believed that she would not die. He felt a deep relief allied to elation.

He moved quickly to the door to see two plainclothes men hurrying along the passage. Once or twice he heard a shot, but no volley followed.

He did not know what to expect, what danger might be waiting. He had believed from the start that Georgette was one of the keys to the mystery, and he meant to get her out of the house safely, letting the rest go hang. He lifted her bodily and carried her to the door, hurrying past the upturned chair near which the unconscious Japanese and his now useless tommy-gun were lying. Moving cautiously down the stairs he saw two uniformed policemen running from the house into the street.

He followed them quickly.

What he saw from the porch made him pull up short, for it was a startling thing.

On the opposite side of Portiman Square was a crowd of people shouting and waving as if in encouragement to people in the sky.

Dawlish walked across the road, still carrying Georgette, and although two or three people saw him they did not give him or his burden a second glance. Once in front of the crowd he turned and looked towards the roof of Number 31 and the houses adjoining.

His eyes narrowed as he watched, and his heart beat fast.

A dozen or more men were moving along the roofs, from one house to another. They were clearly Japanese. Nearer Number 31 the police could be seen following them.

Then Dawlish saw one of the Japanese stationary by a chimney stack. He saw the tommy-gun the man was carrying, and guessed his purpose; he was to delay the pursuit while the others took their chance at escaping. Dawlish shouted at the top of his voice, turned desperately to one side, and saw a constable who was trying to get the crowd to move along.

Dawlish reached him and put Georgette in his arms.

The express of stupefaction on the man's face would have been comic at any other time. Just then Dawlish hardly noticed it as he snapped:

'Look after her, Constable, Inspector Trivett wants her.'

Then he ran towards the corner house, shouting to the police on the roof as he went. He saw that Trivett was at their head, and knew that Trivett could not see the tommy-gun. He fired at the man behind it twice, but succeeded only in dislodging slates in the roof near him.

He could see the set expression on the yellow face, knew that if Trivett did not stop he would be blasted from the roof with a stream of bullets.

Desperately Dawlish aimed for Trivett's legs, saw him stagger, and then begin to slide down the roof.

Dawlish was running towards the house, seeing Trivett falling, seeing also that the men behind him had at last realised the danger and were keeping under cover. Dawlish ignored that: he had eyes only for Trivett as the Inspector slid nearer and nearer to the edge. Dawlish saw his legs beyond the guttering, then his knees, and could only stand and stare upwards with a great sickness within him.

CHAPTER THIRTEEN

GEORGETTE AGAIN

Only seconds passed, but to Dawlish they seemed never-ending. Slowly Trivett's body appeared over the guttering; Dawlish knew that if he fell from the four stories there would be small chance of saving him from serious injury.

Trivett stopped moving.

He was halfway over the edge, and another movement would bring him right down; Dawlish did not seriously think there was a great chance of saving him. But he had to try, and he climbed to the railings outside the house quickly. Its doorway was covered by a square porch with a strong roof. Dawlish reached it, and found he was just able to touch the sill of the window above.

By then others were following him.

He managed to get a grip on the window, and slowly hauled himself up. Once or twice he thought that the weight on his wrists and shoulders would prove too much, but he contrived to haul himself to a position where he was kneeling on the sill; then it was easy to get to his feet on it.

Another sill, another window; and then he might be able to reach Trivett.

He knew that if he succeeded he would be entirely dependent on help from below; but if he could gain time that would be enough. He did not give himself much breathing space, but started the next effort. His fingers tightened on the sill, slowly he hauled his body up. The strain on his arms was so great, the pain so excruciating, that there were moments when he thought that he must relax.

He knew that if he did so, he would fall, that the danger to him was now as great as to Trivett.

He was unconscious of the crowd still lining the pavement and staring up. He did not know that they were breathlessly watching the drama in which he was playing, that lips gaped and voices gasped when he slipped an inch, sighing when he regained it and went on. He was unaware of the fact that at least a hundred people were watching every movement, seeing his large khaki-clad figure climbing laboriously and perilously, yet still a long way beneath his quarry.

Dawlish tightened his lips, hauled again, then slowly got his knee to the sill. He rested there for a moment, then, very slowly, straightened up. Gripping the masonry at the top of the window he stretched upward.

He needed another three or four inches.

There was a groan from the square as slowly he lowered himself, peering through the window into what looked like an empty room. He broke the glass with his elbow, each movement slow, deliberate and painful. He took out several pieces of the broken glass, then climbed through. The room was empty save for two hardwood chairs and some books in a shelf against one wall.

He heard a sudden *tap-tap-tap* above him, and knew that the shooting had started again. He took the larger books, piled them on the window, and then climbed out again. He trod on the pile, afraid every moment that one of the books would slip and pitch him down. Carefully he put his full weight on them, and with the extra height was able to get a hand beneath Trivett's legs.

Then Trivett slipped again.

From the crowd there was a gasp that sounded like a moan carried on a high wind. Dawlish heard it, but was thinking only of the weight which had suddenly descended on his arm. He had a hand about Trivett's right leg just above the knee, but the weight was so great that he did not think he could maintain his hold for more than a few minutes. Sweat was streaming down his face as the pressure increased, until he thought each moment must be the last.

Then there came a cheer from the crowd, a high-pitched, exultant roar. He did not know what caused it, but after a few seconds heard a scraping on the wall near him. Looking towards it he saw the top of a ladder. It moved uncertainly for several seconds, then settled into position. The ladder shook as a man climbed up it, and finally Dawlish saw the top of a steel helmet.

'Now we won't be long, mate,' said a cheerful voice.

The steel-hatted man eased Trivett to his broad back and, with a nonchalance which Dawlish remembered afterwards but at the time hardly noticed, began to climb slowly down.

Dawlish stood there swaying unsteadily, taking in great gulps of air. His position was precarious, but he did not give it much thought, was concerned mainly with getting the circulation back into his arm. It was with sharp surprise that he heard a second voice alongside him, as another steel-hatted man said:

'Lemme give you a n'and, Guv'ner.'

Dawlish turned his head.

'Yes, good idea. I'm afraid of those books slipping.'

'Soon put that right, Guv'ner,' said the newcomer with a wide grin. 'Easy does it, easy—that's the style.'

Carefully Dawlish was helped to a safer position, a feeling of buoyancy slowly taking possession of him. Danger was gone, Trivett was safe, the girl——

Yes, the girl; where was she?

He grew tense, scanning the crowd for a sight of the policeman to whom he had delivered Georgette. He could not see him.

Georgette—where was Georgette?

'What's the trouble?' asked the A.R.P. man perkily. 'Ain't you got no 'ead for 'eights? Don't look dahn, that's the secret. 'Ead 'igh and look up, like the parson says, and you won't 'ave to worry.'

Dawlish smiled briefly.

'I'm all right. I'm looking for——'

He stopped abruptly, seeing a stretcher being loaded into an ambulance with the figure of a girl on it. Despite the distance he was sure that it was Georgette. A policeman was superintending her removal, and Dawlish, his mind at rest, settled back against the window.

'Well, wot abaht it?' demanded the A.R.P. warden. 'Nice view up 'ere, but it's a bit chilly.' He measured Dawlish's bulk with a speculative eye, adding: 'Say, chum, I don't mind tryin', but I ain't guaranteein' I'll carry yer dahn. A bit over my weight, you are.'

Dawlish chuckled.

'All right, I'll carry you.'

'No fear you don't,' said the other, descending two rungs of the ladder hastily. 'Strewth, the boys wouldn't arf 'ave the laugh on me then.'

Dawlish chuckled again. 'All right, let's make it.'

'I'll tell yer one thing,' declared the steel-hatted one, 'you're a cool customer, all right. But don't go taking no chances, this ladder wasn't built fer a ton weight. Take it easy, an' follow me.'

Nearing ground level, Dawlish turned to view the dwindling crowd. Then he stiffened, for he saw Simon J. Simon standing far back. Not two yards from him was Felicity.

Simon caught his eye.

The man gave no sign of recognition, but turned abruptly away. Felicity did not wait to attract Dawlish's attention, but followed Simon.

Dawlish knew that there was no chance at all of getting through the crowd in time to reach her. But anxiety sprang into his mind, and would increase until Felicity had returned.

Felicity had not telephoned, nor returned, by seven o'clock that evening.

For Dawlish the intervening hours had been busy, although throughout them he felt a nagging anxiety for Felicity; he did not believe Simon would remain long in ignorance of the fact that he was being followed. Even the rush of events, or rather of explanations, did little to erase this anxiety.

Yet there were causes for satisfaction.

Georgette Wilson was at the same hospital as Trivett. Dawlish saw Trivett first, learning for the first time that his bullet had glanced off the sole of Trivett's shoe, causing him to lose his balance, though saving him from the blast of the tommy-gun.

'They've told me what you did, Pat,' he said. 'I'm not going to waste your time or mine trying to say thanks. Except, well, thanks.'

Dawlish smiled. 'I brought you down, so I had to keep you up. You haven't heard any more about the little men at Porti-

83

man Square, I suppose?'

'Nothing beyond the fact that they all got clear.'

'Bad show,' said Dawlish. 'I haven't got it straight in my head yet.'

'I haven't got anything straight,' Trivett grumbled. 'It's just one damned thing after another, each a little more inconclusive than the last.'

'Have a heart,' said Dawlish with a certain relish. 'We've only just started.'

'Curse you,' said Trivett with a grin, 'why didn't I think of taking a pot shot at your number nines? Let me know what happens, won't you?'

'I will,' promised Dawlish, and meant it.

From Trivett's ward he went to the telephone and tried, without success, to contact Sir Archibald Morely, the Assistant Commissioner at Scotland Yard and Trivett's Chief. He then went on to see Georgette.

Her large eyes widened at the sight of him.

'Hallo,' said Dawlish amiably. 'How are tricks?'

Georgette eased herself up in bed, looked towards the door and then at the bell-push by her side, as if to summon help. It was obvious to Dawlish that she was not going to be helpful if she could avoid it. He was puzzled by the variety of attitudes adopted by the girl in the past two days. Which of them were genuine?

'What do you want?' she demanded.

'Information,' said Dawlish laconically.

'I can tell you nothing.'

'No?' Dawlish raised an eyebrow. 'You mean won't, of course. Georgette——'

She said freezingly: 'I don't want to talk to you.'

'Indeed? Then I take it you would prefer to be put under arrest and charged with murder?'

If Dawlish's manner was casual his mental alertness was not. He saw that she was surprised but not afraid. He believed that had she been guilty of murder, or any part in it, she would have betrayed a momentary glimpse of fear.

She said sharply: 'And what do you mean by that?'

Dawlish shrugged.

'I was able to delay the police call on you by an hour. If I hadn't done so you would be under arrest by now.'

'Don't be a fool,' said Georgette. 'You can't frighten me that way. Who do they think I killed?'

'The Rt. Hon. Horatio Chumley,' said Dawlish lightly, 'whom you visited last night after sending him a note regretting that you couldn't see him.'

He had all the effect he wanted then.

He saw her stiffen at the mention of Chumley, watched the expression of alarm, even horror, that sprang to her eyes.

'*Chumley,*' she breathed. '*He's* dead?'

'He is indeed,' said Dawlish with deliberate coldness, 'a fact which you knew even before I did. Surely you hadn't forgotten?'

'I didn't! I didn't!' The words came harshly from lips whitened in shock.

She was at bay, he knew, fighting against fear, against horror, and above all against him.

He looked at her, his face expressionless.

'You visited him last night. He was poisoned during the night. That's going to be hard to explain, Georgette.'

'He was alive when I left him!' she threw at him, 'he was as well as he's ever been! I only went because he telephoned me, he wanted to try to get more information, he wanted——'

'What did he find out about you?' demanded Dawlish. 'What did he tell you that made you want to kill him?'

'I didn't kill him!' she flared. 'You're trying to trap me! I know nothing about it! He——'

She stopped abruptly, looking over Dawlish's shoulder towards the door. From the corner of his eye Dawlish saw that a man was standing there. He turned without haste to find himself looking into the white face and feverish eyes of Gerald North.

In his right hand was an automatic.

CHAPTER FOURTEEN

TRUTH OR LIES?

Dawlish eyed the gun with some trepidation. He did not like the feverishness in the man's eyes. It was the kind of look which both juries and coroners called temporary insanity.

He said easily: 'What's this, North? How did you get in here?'

'Never mind that,' said North thickly. 'Get up, Georgette.'

'Stay where you are,' said Dawlish.

North snarled: 'Keep your mouth shut, Dawlish!' He was drunk, but not drunk enough to make the mistake of shouting. 'Georgette, get up. You're coming with me.'

Dawlish backed towards the wall alongside Georgette's bed. From her expression he imagined that her earlier emotions had faded into nervousness—fear was perhaps too great a word— at North's appearance.

Leaning against the wall, Dawlish felt the bell-push with his left hip.

He pressed it.

Aloud, he said pleasantly: 'North, this won't get you any-where, you know. The police have the hospital under guard, they want Miss Wilson for questioning, and they also want you. You were a fool to come here.'

'I know what I'm doing,' said North. 'I don't want to have to talk to you again. Georgette——'

He took a step nearer the bed. Georgette pushed the clothes on one side and swung her feet to the floor. Dawlish believed she was more afraid of North and the gun than she had been of the threat of arrest.

For the first time since North's arrival she spoke.

'My clothes aren't here.'

'Look in that cupboard,' North said, jerking his free hand towards a cupboard set against the far wall. 'We haven't any time to lose. Hurry!'

Dawlish watched the man's face working.

The frankness he had seen that afternoon was now covered by an expression of fear. Dawlish did not try to find any explanation, but accepted it as yet another development which would have to be worked out before the end was reached. He wondered how long it would be before someone came in response to his ring. Footsteps sounded in the passage.

North stiffened.

The handle of the door turned. North swung round before the door opened, and on that moment Dawlish moved.

In a split second he had covered the ground between himself and North, striking him on the side of the jaw with a force which sent the man skidding to the floor. Seizing the gun he backed away.

The nurse and Georgette both stood in petrified silence, then professionalism swung into command and the nurse snapped:

'Get back to bed at once!'

Dawlish smiled at her reassuringly.

'I think we're all right now, nurse. I believe there's a Sergeant Munk in the hospital somewhere. Could you get him?'

The nurse turned and hurried away, while Dawlish looked at North and then Georgette. North stared back at him dully, and the large man frowned; was it possible that North was drugged and not drunk?

Dawlish said: 'If you two have any sense at all, you'll listen to me and do what I say. The policeman coming now has instructions to watch you both, and to make sure you don't get away again. I think I can persuade him to let me take you to my flat, but if you start threatening or blustering it won't be possible.'

He stopped as the door opened more widely.

Detective Sergeant Munk entered, bellicose of aspect, his fierce moustache bristling as if filled with its possessor's righteous anger.

'Now what's up?' he demanded truculently. 'You, what are you doing 'ere?' He glared at North.

North kept silent.

'Sergeant——' began Dawlish.

'Now listen 'ere,' said Sergeant Munk, after a sigh suggesting that his patience would rapidly be exhausted. 'I want to 'elp you, Mr. Dawlish, but we can't 'ave things going on like this. That nurse was fair scared. Guns all over the place, she said, and patients getting out o' bed when they want to. It won't do. Besides——'

'Your turn to be interrupted,' said Dawlish amiably. 'There was a misunderstanding, Sergeant. Miss Wilson is well enough to leave here, now, and I've suggested that they both come to my flat for a talk about the general situation.'

'Oh no, they don't,' said Munk.

Dawlish said wheedlingly: 'They'll be safe enough with me, Sergeant.'

'That's what you *think*,' declared Munk, 'but not necessarily what *I* do. I've 'ad my instructions, Mr. Dawlish, and I sticks to them.'

'What instructions are they?' asked Georgette.

'Never you mind,' said Munk. 'I've got 'em, and I sticks to 'em. I want a word with Mr. North at the station, I want to know what he was doing 'ere, *and* where he's been today. A lot of funny things 'ave 'appened,' went on Munk. He turned fiercely towards Dawlish. 'And if it comes to that, I've got a lot o' questions to ask *you*, sir.'

Dawlish said: 'They can be questioned at my flat as well as at the station, and they won't try to run away. I'll give you my word on it.'

Munk stared at him without speaking, and then his right eyelid flickered in a wink so quick that only Dawlish noticed it.

'Just you wait 'ere,' he said. 'I'll be back soon, and remember there's a man outside the door, I ain't taking any more chances.' He sniffed fiercely and went out, leaving a silent trio behind him.

Dawlish saw that Munk's manner had driven the inertia from North, and had really frightened Georgette. Inwardly he smiled, although he remained puzzled; they showed a naïveté which surely did not belong to anyone who was deeply involved in four murders.

'Well?' Georgette asked tensely.

'I'll see what I can do,' said Dawlish.

'You must do something!' snapped North. 'It's nonsense to arrest us, we've done nothing wrong!'

'No?' Dawlish asked. 'Nevertheless, you're going to have a hard job to explain yourselves. What were the Japanese doing at the house, for instance?'

'I don't know!' North shouted.

'Oh, come. You're a resident there, and you were in charge, weren't you?'

'No, I wasn't! I'd been out most of the day with Georgette. I hadn't been back half an hour when you arrived and started knocking me about!'

Dawlish said: 'We needn't hold an inquest on that. Why didn't you let me see Georgette?'

'She was worn out, she needed a rest.'

'She was certainly having one,' said Dawlish dryly. 'If I'd arrived five minutes later she'd have been strangled in her own bed.'

'She—what?' gasped North.

'You heard. Why do you think her neck's bandaged? Why——' He paused, raising a hand resignedly. 'What is the use of talking? You're both in trouble as deep as you can go. You're to be charged with conspiring in the attempted murder of Georgette, North, and Georgette is to be charged with the murder of Chumley.'

The half-truths came smoothly and convincingly. He had them both frightened.

Munk returned before either of them replied.

'Straight to your flat, Mr. Dawlish, that's all,' he said, his sniff registering disapproval. 'I'll be there myself before long, don't make any mistake about it.'

Dawlish and North waited in the passage while Georgette dressed.

Dawlish did not think either North or the girl would lie easily when they reached the flat. They were as scared as he had wanted them to be. His anxiety was whether their story would be useful and could clear up any of the outstanding mysteries, or whether it would make the confusion even greater.

It was seven o'clock when the three of them reached Jermyn Street.

The policeman who had been on duty at the flat had nothing to report, thus giving Dawlish more worry about Felicity. There was a general police call out for her, and for Simon, but the knowledge of that did not make him feel any happier.

Dawlish ushered Georgette to an easy chair.

The short journey by taxi had not worried her, and the doctor at the hospital had assured him that she had recovered quickly and completely from the attempted strangling, and that there was no danger of a relapse. He was puzzled because she did not seem to be perturbed by the fact that she had been so near to death. He believed that her concern was not for herself but for something or someone else.

North, refusing to sit down, paced the floor.

'Now look here, Dawlish, we've got to get the thing straight. It's absolute nonsense to talk about Georgette murdering Chumley. And you're not in your right senses if you think I knew anything about the attack on her. Damn it, we've been engaged for over a year!'

Dawlish's eyebrows rose.

'Openly or secretly?' he inquired, for he had heard nothing of such an engagement before.

'We've kept it to ourselves, but I don't see what that's got to do with it,' said North abruptly. 'Her father didn't approve because he thought she was too young; there was no other reason. We've nothing to be ashamed of, and nothing to hide.'

Dawlish said: 'You've been hiding plenty.'

North turned abruptly to the girl.

'Georgette, I can speak for you, can't I? I don't want to say anything you don't want said. Would you rather tell the story?'

Georgette shook her head. North's voice had held appeal, and he was clearly relieved that she left the telling to him. Before he went on, however, Dawlish said quietly:

'North, you must get this into your head. Everything you know has to be told, whether it appears to incriminate you or whether it doesn't. The issues at stake are too large for any personal anxieties to be allowed to intrude. We'll get the truth,' he added evenly, 'no matter how long it takes. But the quicker the better, for you, for me, and probably for a lot of people we don't know. Now then, we'll make it orderly, I'll ask questions and you can answer. First——' He paused, to let his opening words sink in. 'First of all, why did you tell the Press that Professor Wilson was going to take a rest in the country when you knew quite well that he proposed to ignore the threats and continue working?'

CHAPTER FIFTEEN

PARTLY CLEAR?

North said stubbornly: 'Because that is what he told me to say.'

'That's right,' Georgette put in. 'Father decided that it would be wise to make it seem that he was obeying. I suggested it.'

'Oh,' said Dawlish, feeling a little deflated. He had hoped to create a sensation, and instead North and Georgette were unanimous in an assertion which certainly could not now be denied by Professor Wilson. 'Did anyone else know?' he asked.

'Yes, both the other secretaries,' said North.

'And their names?'

'Peter Fuelling and Mr. Arthurson.' North paused. 'Peter's about my age, Arthurson is a much older man. I did the general correspondence and some minor figure work, helped by Georgette. Peter's a mathematical wizard, and Arthurson is an economic expert. He was almost a partner, although officially one of the Professor's secretaries.'

'Were either of them at Portiman Square today?' asked Dawlish, feeling his way slowly and beginning to doubt whether he had been wrong to concentrate on this couple. The more he looked at the position the more he realised that he had overlooked many things.

'No,' said North. 'Arthurson has gone up north, as a representative of the Professor, to a meeting of some economic advisers to the government. Peter Fuelling took a load of work home with him. He does more work at home than he does at Portiman Square.'

'Hmm,' said Dawlish, and rubbed his nose. The two secretaries might prove to be dead-ends, he reflected, but on the other hand North might be deliberately side-tracking him. 'All right, we'll go on a bit. The Professor visited Lord Breddon with some information of exceptional importance, and also told him of the threats. Right?'

'I've told you that once,' said Georgette impatiently.

'There are things I can bear hearing twice,' said Dawlish. 'I suppose it's occurred to neither of you that I'm doing my damndest to help you?'

Neither of them spoke, and he went on in an uncomfortable silence:

'Lord Breddon reported the matter to Chumley, and in turn to Colonel Cranton. Was that the procedure?'

'Yes,' said Georgette unexpectedly. 'Lord Breddon knew Mr. Chumley well, that's why he went to him.'

'Good. How well did you know Chumley?' Dawlish asked.

She said sharply: 'The first time I met him was about a week ago. What are you driving at?'

'The truth, I hope. How did you come to meet him?'

'I was at Lord Breddon's house for luncheon,' said Georgette, 'and we met there.' She hesitated, and then went on: 'Mr. Chumley invited me to a theatre and dinner, the next night. I did not accept. I had several other invitations from him, but refused them all on the score of being busy. It was difficult,' she added with heightened colour. 'Gerald didn't like me dining with other men, and none of them knew that we were engaged.'

'Hmm, well, did you see Chumley after your first meeting, before you visited him last night?'

'No, but he wrote to me two or three times. Each time I sent him a little note in reply,' Georgette added, 'getting more definite each time. Then last evening he telephoned me at Portiman Square, and said he wanted to see me about Father's —death. I'd taken it for granted the last letter, received yesterday afternoon, had been just another invitation, but I knew that it wasn't when he telephoned. That's why I went.'

Dawlish said: 'Where did he telephone you?'

'At Portiman Square.'

'You weren't seen to return there yesterday,' said Dawlish. 'In fact you had us worried, we didn't know where you'd gone. Why did you leave Salisbury so suddenly?'

Georgette said fiercely: 'I hated the place, I detested you and your friends, I blamed you for what had happened. I just had to get away, and I took the chance when it offered. I caught a train to London, and went home by cab. It was dark, and I went in the back way. I just didn't want to be seen. I was afraid that reporters might be waiting for me. That's reasonable enough, isn't it?' she demanded sharply. 'Will the police argue about that?'

'They'll probably want proof,' Dawlish said.

'I can supply it,' said North quickly. 'Georgette phoned me and asked me to meet the train, but I found several reporters outside and they started to follow me. I knew she wouldn't want to see them, and came back. I was waiting when she arrived.'

'Who else was there?'

'Only the servants. Look here, Dawlish——' North's first drunken emotionalism having worn itself out, Dawlish was pleased to sense a calmer and more reasonable attitude. 'It has been a devil of a blow to Georgette, and to me. We'd known the Professor was worried, but we'd no idea what it was about until Georgette read the threatening letters. Then things happened so damn fast that we hardly knew where we were.'

'I'd had time to think in the train,' said Georgette. 'I saw then that we had to help to find the man who'd killed father. That's all I thought about, all Gerald thought about.'

'Well?' asked Dawlish.

'We thought about it and talked about it,' said Georgette, 'and then the call came from Chumley. I went to see him, going out the back way again to deceive the reporters. They waited all night, and kept asking for an interview. Gerald kept them occupied at the front door while I went out, and then he followed me. He was waiting for me when I left Chumley's flat.'

'At what time?' asked Dawlish.

'It must have been about one o'clock,' said North. 'I know it was perishing cold. Georgette came out in a hurry, and told me that Chumley hadn't been able to tell her much, he was hoping she could tell him more about what the Professor was working on.'

'And couldn't she?' flashed Dawlish.

'I'd no more idea than Chumley,' said Georgette slowly. 'He was very sweet, and—oh well, what is the use of talking about that now? I'd no idea he was in danger, he was quite cheerful when I saw him, and seemed confident enough that he would soon learn what it was about, and who the murderers were.' She paused, and then said stiffly: 'I told him that I'd met you, and didn't think much of what you'd done. He told me that I could rely on you to get results.'

Dawlish said: 'That was nice of him, Georgette.' He spoke quite simply and without irony. 'I do try, you know, but you didn't help. We've lost valuable time, and there are a lot of things outstanding even now. For instance, what happened this morning?'

'I was in my room most of the morning,' Georgette said.

'I hung about the house,' said North.

'You had a lot of visitors,' Dawlish said quietly. 'What business were they on?'

North stared at him. 'Visitors? There were some reporters, and one or two friends called to offer their condolences. That's all.'

Dawlish said: 'Think again, North. The police were watching the house all the time. Twenty-five men, if not more, entered the house and didn't leave it again as far as the police could see.'

'Nonsense!' exclaimed North.

'Fact,' insisted Dawlish.

'I don't believe it,' said Georgette crisply. 'We saw everyone who called—or at least, Gerald did, and he told me of them as soon as they'd gone.'

Dawlish looked from one to the other, trying to decide whether they were lying, and hoping to get away with it, or whether in fact they really did know nothing of the men who had entered 31 Portiman Square. There was more than that at issue, moreover; he was quite sure that the men the police had seen had not been Japanese; yet the only men he had seen on the visit to the house had been Japs, except for North and the servant.

'It's true, I tell you,' North insisted. 'I had the shock of my life when I learnt there were people upstairs.'

'Are you trying to tell me that over twenty men met at the house while you were there, and you had no knowledge of it?' Dawlish demanded.

'It's true!' declared Georgette. 'However mad it sounds, it's true. All the servants were away, except Grey, as Father expected to be in Salisbury for some days. Grey—*Grey* wouldn't have let those people in!'

'Someone did,' said Dawlish, 'and they went in by the front door.'

North drew a deep breath, eyeing Georgette with a confusion so convincing that Dawlish was impressed. Georgette lifted her hands, and then they said together:

'I suppose——' began Georgette.

'Grey could——' started North.

Dawlish put in swiftly: 'Grey could have admitted them while you were both upstairs, and they could have gone through the servants' quarters and up the back stairs. Grey would have been in the conspiracy, and assuming he was, they could have got there without your knowledge.'

'But twenty five of them!' exclaimed North.

'It's fantastic!' declared Georgette. 'I just can't believe it!'

Dawlish glanced at his watch. It was eight o'clock, and he was reminded of the swift passing of time by the fact that he was both hungry and thirsty. The glance reminded him abruptly that Felicity was still missing. For a few seconds his thoughts wandered, but he collected himself and went on quietly.

'It happened, you've got to take that as certain. Have there

95

been any other occasions when a crowd of men met at the house?'

'Yes,' said North quickly.

'Often,' said Georgette.

'Who and when?' asked Dawlish.

'There were conferences,' North told him, 'in the ballroom, at least three times a month. The Professor believed in a general exchange of views as often as they could be obtained. He always made a summary of what was said, and based his reports on that. The reports went through to Lord Breddon.'

'And did Grey always let these people in?'

'Grey was usually on duty, yes.'

'Normally they went up the main staircase, of course,' mused Dawlish, 'but for this special occasion they wouldn't do that. It was nicely arranged, that's obvious now. Unless the police had been worrying about you and Georgette, no one would have reported the gathering at Number 31, it was too usual an occurrence. Tell me, was a man named Simon ever in attendance?'

'Simon J. Simon, do you mean?' asked North.

'Oh yes, he was often there,' Georgette put in. 'I had lunch with him today, as a matter of fact. Why do you name him specifically?'

'Because he's been to see me,' said Dawlish, eyeing the girl curiously. *Was* she really as ingenuous as she seemed? 'Where did you go after lunching with him? And why didn't you tell me you had been out? You gave me the impression that you'd been in all day.' He omitted to mention that he had seen her lunching.

Georgette said sharply: 'I can't help what wrong impressions you get. We both lunched with Simon.'

'Is that usual?' demanded Dawlish.

'We've often had a meal with him at his Club,' said North. 'He's a decent sort of fellow, brilliant in his way. He hasn't many friends, and I happened to be able to help him once or twice. I don't like refusing when he invites me to lunch or dinner, and today was rather a special event, anyhow. He had told us that he knew of the threats, and that he worked with Colonel Cranton. We went because'—North sought for the

96

right word—'well, because we were keyed up pretty high, and wanted to find out whether he could tell us anything. After all, if he worked with Cranton there was a reasonable chance that he could.'

'Yes,' said Dawlish.

It was all plausible enough, and they had made no attempt to hide the fact that both had been at the Aliens' Club. He wondered whether it was possible that either of them knew of the attack on him. He thought it unlikely but found his mind straying on the real reason for it. Kori Oroshu had not told the whole truth, and Dawlish was quite sure that he had been shanghaied with one object; to keep him at the Club for an hour or more.

There was also the matter of Tim Jeremy's injury.

'Did either of you leave with Simon?' Dawlish asked.

'We both did,' said Georgette.

'Where did you go?'

'We walked straight home,' said North. 'Simon left us in Piccadilly. I understood he was going to one of the government offices in Whitehall. Why all these questions about him?'

'We'll worry about that later,' said Dawlish. 'Did either of you notice that you were followed from the Club?'

North snapped: 'Followed? Who by?'

'A tall man in an officer's uniform.'

'Yes, I noticed him!' exclaimed Georgette excitedly. 'Don't you remember, Gerry? I told you I thought I'd seen him at Salisbury.'

'Was Simon with you then?' asked Dawlish.

'Oh yes, it was just after we left the Club. Who was he?' Georgette paused a moment, and then went on: 'I've got it! He was a friend of yours! So you knew all along that we'd been to the Aliens' Club for lunch.'

'Let's stick to the point,' said Dawlish tersely. 'Did you see him after you left Simon?'

'I didn't look,' said Georgette.

'Nor did I,' North said positively. 'Look here, Dawlish, you said just now that you were trying to help us. I don't think so much of the way you do it. Who made the police suspicious of us, if it wasn't you?'

Dawlish said: 'The police don't need my help to make them suspicious, and they always get the facts. Your only safe course with them is the truth and the whole truth, no matter how difficult it might make things look for you.'

'I'm beginning to wonder,' said Georgette slowly, 'whether you haven't tricked us into telling you what we have, whether you won't report it to the police.'

'Why shouldn't they know?' countered Dawlish sharply.

'There's no reason, except——' She broke off in confusion, and then added hastily: 'It's a beastly way of doing things, scaring us first and then making us talk while pretending you're friendly.'

'The day may dawn when you'll realise just how friendly it was to make you talk,' said Dawlish. 'As for what the police do now, that's up to them. I don't think they'll want you in cells, provided you don't try to lose yourselves. Now, a last question. Do you know anything of what the Professor was working on—beyond a vague generalisation?'

'No,' said North emphatically.

'I think he'd learnt *something*, but he wouldn't say what it was,' Georgette declared.

'Did *anyone* know—before he passed it on to Breddon and Cranton?' Dawlish demanded.

'Arthurson might have known something about it,' North said, 'but it isn't certain by any means. Look here, how long are you going to keep us here?'

'Until the police have seen you again,' said Dawlish crisply, and glanced at his wrist-watch. It was a quarter to nine. He frowned, and a mental image of Felicity appeared in his mind's eye. Felicity, in Simon's wake. If Simon had tried to poison him, and he had not doubted that at the time, then Simon had probably handled Tim Jeremy brutally, and had doubtless made arrangements with Kori Oroshu; was it likely that Felicity would escape the man's attentions?

Dawlish thought on those lines, while North and Georgette watched him, saying nothing. He stood up abruptly, and his voice was gruff.

'We may as well see what's in the larder, anyhow.'

'I'm not hungry,' Georgette said.

'I couldn't eat if I tried,' North said brusquely. 'You seem to me to be taking this business far too calmly, Dawlish.'

'Oh,' said Dawlish. 'Calmly?' He shrugged, and then went to the kitchen, leaving the door open so that he could watch the couple unobserved. They sat in silence for a moment, and then North leaned across to Georgette and whispered something. Georgette nodded.

From the kitchen, Dawlish said: 'Were all the economists who met at Portiman Square English?'

'No,' said North testily. 'Simon isn't, and we've told you he was often there. I don't suppose more than half of them were English. There are brains in other countries, you know.'

Dawlish, cutting bread, asked which countries were usually represented at the Conferences, and was told that there were Germans, Austrians, Italians, French, Dutch and Belgians, always two or three Americans, an Indian and several Chinese. He had never seen a Japanese there, although he would not swear that he could always tell the difference between a Jap and a Chinaman.

Dawlish finished making a cheese sandwich which he started to eat, after the others had repeated that they would not join him. They were glad of coffee, however, which North helped to prepare.

The atmosphere, being by now somewhat relaxed, Dawlish said casually:

'There's one other thing, North. Why did you try to get Georgette away from the hospital? Hadn't you the sense to know that it was crazy?'

North coloured. 'I'd had one too many,' he said, 'and I was worried, I knew that Chumley's murder had taken place last night and that it must have looked bad for Georgette. I wanted to warn her, and I didn't see a chance of doing it while she remained at the hospital. That's all there is in it.'

'All?' Dawlish asked, his eyebrows raised. 'Why did you have a gun with you?'

'I thought I could scare anyone who interfered,' muttered North. 'I must have seemed a damn fool.'

'Drink is considered to be an excuse for that,' said Dawlish drily. 'Georgette, did you know who attacked you this afternoon?'

Georgette shook her head. 'I couldn't see who it was, they put a cloth over my face. I don't think I was conscious very long.' She gave an involuntary shudder. 'It was a ghastly few minutes. Who got me away?'

'Let him remain anonymous,' said Dawlish. 'I wish——' He broke off abruptly.

'What do you wish?' North demanded.

'That Felicity would turn up,' Dawlish said.

He imagined that Georgette understood something of what he was feeling.

After another ten minutes of waiting, the front door bell rang.

Dawlish strode to the door, his hands fumbling at the catch. He heard a faint thud outside, and was filled with sudden alarm. He had the door open at last, and in the light of the hall saw Felicity.

Her cheeks were bloodless, her lips agape, her breathing stertorous. She did not appear to recognise him, but swayed forward suddenly, leaning her full weight against him.

Dawlish said: 'Oh my God!' and lifted her into his arms.

She said something incoherently, tried to repeat it, and then her head fell back and she lost consciousness.

CHAPTER SIXTEEN

WHERE IS MR. SIMON?

Dawlish carried Felicity into the bedroom, speaking over his shoulder as he went.

'Telephone Dr. Miller at once, one of you. South Audley Street.' He heard both North and Georgette moving towards the telephone as he laid Felicity gently onto the bed. He did not doubt—for she had no apparent injury—that she had been drugged heavily and within the past hour or two; he had seen morphia injections which had taken a similar effect.

He took off her shoes, and then Georgette entered quietly.

'Can I help you?' she said.

'Thanks,' said Dawlish. 'Is Dr. Miller coming?'

'He said he wouldn't be more than twenty minutes,' Georgette assured him. She leant over Felicity. 'You needn't stay,' she said pointedly.

Dawlish hesitated. Georgette was capable, and it was absurd to suspect that she would try to do Felicity any further harm, he told himself. He turned reluctantly towards the lounge.

He found North by the telephone.

'I say, Dawlish, I'm damned sorry about this,' he mumbled.

'Thanks. One way and the other, the enemy is efficient. I haven't even got to grips with the swine yet. But I will.' Dawlish stared at North until the latter coloured uncomfortably. 'Yes, I will,' Dawlish repeated, and stepped forward, picking up the telephone. He dialled *Inquiries*, asking for the number of the Royal Hotel, Amesbury.

There was some delay before he was through, but at last he heard the voice of a receptionist saying:

'Royal Hotel, Amesbury.'

'I wish to speak to Lady Blake.'

'Hold on one moment, sir, please.'

Dawlish shifted his position so that he could see Felicity's bed. Georgette had apparently removed her clothes, for he could see them flung over a chair. He cursed under his breath without ceasing, until Hermina Blake's voice sounded in his ear.

'Hallo, who's that?'

'Dawlish. Is Ted Beresford still around, Hermina? It's urgent.'

'I saw him before dinner,' said Hermina, 'but it'll be five minutes before I can get him over here. He's staying at——'

'A message will do,' interrupted Dawlish. 'Ask him to get to London, and the flat, as soon as he can.'

Hermina's voice rose in surprise.

'But what about the couple down here, Pat?'

'What are they doing?'

'They're just hanging around,' said Hermina, a little help-lessly, 'playing bridge and reading the papers. I'm beginning to wonder whether you're right in thinking they know any-thing. Even Ted seems to think it's a waste of time.'

'He could be right,' said Dawlish grimly. 'But they want watching. Tell Freddie to keep his eyes open until he hears from the local police. I'll try to make some arrangements with them to replace Ted. Sorry to be abrupt, but time's precious.'

'Yes, but wait a minute!' Hermina cried. 'Pat, how's that poor girl, Georgette? I've wondered such a lot about her.'

'Doing fine,' said Dawlish. 'I really can't stay, Hermina. Apologies now and explanations later.'

He replaced the receiver, to find North eyeing him and Georgette putting hot-water bottles into Felicity's bed. He did not know whether to feel grateful towards Georgette for her practical nursing, or whether to blame her for what had hap-pened. He knew that he was not only on edge but in a mood in which he could easily do the wrong thing.

Then three people called, one after the other.

The first was Dr. Miller, who had hardly reached the bed-room before the bell rang again, and Dawlish opened the door to admit Detective Sergeant Munk. Munk was making signs that he wanted to speak to Dawlish alone, when there was a third ring.

'I'll see who it is,' said North.

Munk whispered: 'Thought you'd better know that the A.C.'s coming tonight, Mr. Dawlish, thought I'd better warn yer. I won't stay.' He moved away from Dawlish as he finished, but stopped abruptly, his expression of anxiety rapidly chang-ing to one of respectful subservience. The only man who in-spired that in Sergeant Munk, to Dawlish's knowledge, was the Assistant Commissioner.

It was, indeed, the A.C., who nodded thanks to North and stepped quickly into the lounge, saw Munk, and frowned.

'What are you doing here, Munk?'

'Just called to see that everything was okay, sir. Thought I'd better, things being 'ow they are.'

'H'm, yes,' said Sir Archibald Morely. 'Always on the spot, aren't you? Wait for me outside, please.'

'Yes, sir,' said Munk, and beat a hasty retreat.

Dawlish smiled grimly as he shook hands with Morely, who was his second cousin. A tall, spare man, looking more than his forty-one years, his manner could be abrupt. It was abrupt then.

'What's the conclave for, Pat?'

'Quite a lot of reasons,' said Dawlish. 'The first one being Felicity. Someone's drugged her.' He took Morely by the arm and led him towards the bedroom. Miller's voice, still speaking to Georgette, drifted out to them.

'You did quite rightly. Keep her warm, and if she shows any signs of coming round give her plenty of hot, strong coffee.' The doctor turned at Dawlish's entrance, his tired eyes ignoring Morely. 'Morphine, Dawlish. How heavy I don't know, but there's every indication that it's not too much. I'll look in again before midnight or a little after. Don't bother, I'll find my way out.'

He did not need to, for North opened the door for him. It flashed across Dawlish's mind that North was little better than a door-boy; it was the first humorous thought he had felt since Felicity had arrived, and was due entirely to Miller's reassuring opinion of Felicity's condition. Dawlish spoke in a quick undertone to Morely.

'Do you want the girl and North detained?'

'What are your ideas?' asked Morely.

'There are men outside to tail them, I take it?'

'Yes.'

'Then I'd let them go.'

Morely nodded. 'All right. But they'd better not do any more harm, or there'll be trouble at the Yard.' He bowed distantly to Georgette. North, by this time, had returned, and Dawlish, turning to him, said with a disarming smile:

'Sergeant Munk looked in to say there's nothing more he needs from you at the moment, but he assumes that you will be staying at Portiman Square.'

'Where else can we stay?' demanded North.

'I don't know,' said Dawlish, 'but if you do decide to go to a hotel, please advise the police before booking rooms.'

'Damn the police,' muttered North.

To disguise the remark Georgette extended a hand to Dawlish.

'You've been very good. I hope that—that it it won't be long before it's cleared up, and we can breath freely again.'

'I don't think it will be too long,' said Dawlish.

He saw them out, and then returned to Morely, frowning irritably.

'You're sure they'll be covered?'

'Damn it, man, I'm not taking more chances,' exploded Morely. 'Be yourself, Pat.'

'That's the trouble, I can't,' said Dawlish. 'I haven't time. I should think she'd be all right, but——' He stopped and shrugged, then went on: 'Twelve hours, it ought to be safe for that time.'

'What are you talking about?' demanded Morely.

'Georgette and North,' said Dawlish. 'Archie, this is a queer show, a *damned* queer show. I've developed an uncomfortable feeling that I know why Georgette was nearly strangled this afternoon, but I can't do everything at once and certainly I can't stay in her bedroom, which would be the only way of making sure she's safe.'

'I've gathered from Trivett that you've a Georgette complex in this business,' Morely said bluntly. 'I don't know what explanation she's given you, but to be sufficient it has to be pretty good. The evidence against her for the Chumley murder is pretty damning. A supply of adrenalin was found in her room at Portiman Square.'

'Was it, by God! And adrenalin in concentrated form was delivered to Chumley, and reacted so strongly on his heart that it killed him. Same with Breddon. Georgette had the opportunity both times, and the stuff is found in her room. That's strong evidence indeed, Archie. Yet you prefer to take my advice and let her go.'

'Yes,' said Morely. 'But there are other considerations. There must be more in it than Georgette Wilson, and, free, she might lead us to them. What story did you get from her about the men at the house? And from North?'

Dawlish said: 'At once unbelievable and plausible. You will probably call me a fool for swallowing it, and yet——' He paused, frowning a little, and then went on to repeat what the couple had told him. As he did so he saw scepticism growing on Morely's face.

Morely said at last: 'Well, Pat, it's the weakest story I've heard for a long time. You surely didn't take it as gospel? Damn it, you couldn't have done!'

'Some of it,' objected Dawlish, 'only some of it. The particular point that worries me is Simon. He was *au fait* with Wilson's arrangements, he claims to have worked with Cranton——'

'He has done, often,' said Morely.

'Cranton isn't the man to back a loser,' Dawlish mused. 'But in Simon's trail many grim things have happened, including—but damn it, now Georgette's gone I need a nurse for Felicity.'

He was busy on the telephone for five minutes, then returned to Morely. A quick look at Felicity showed him that though she was still unconscious her colour was better and her breathing even.

He lowered himself into a chair and looked up at the Assistant Commissioner.

'That's how it's been all along. Something starts, another show cuts across it, and while I'm having a look at the second the first fades away. It's the most elusive business I've played any part in.'

Morely shrugged, making no comment.

Dawlish said: 'It's not only the murders, or the fact that we haven't pinned any one of them on to the killers yet. It's as if no one really knows anything that matters.'

Morely pulled at his upper lip glumly.

'That's about right, Pat. When they put Cranton out they started the show, and when Chumley went they made quite sure that no one in Whitehall *did* know. McKye gave you a different impression, I gather,' added the A.C., not without some satisfaction. 'He stalled, because he doesn't know either. He kept you on it because he's worried. All of them are worried, but none, not even McKye, really believes it's as big as Cranton made out. It's happening in England, and they can't conceive that anything really outstanding can happen here, from the inside. That's the position as I see it. Incidentally,

105

the Home Secretary sees it the same way. I've just come from him.'

Dawlish stirred restlessly in his chair.

'I wonder how long it will be before Cranton can talk?'

'Not for several days,' Morely said. 'I've been on the phone to the hospital. He's not doing well, there's more than a chance of pneumonia, I gather. If this show's to end quickly, you've got to do it.'

'That's too modest,' said Dawlish quickly. 'Even you don't really believe it. But Archie, if there are things we don't know, there are also things we suspect. I asked Trivett to look deeply into the personnel of the Aliens' Club, staff and members.'

'There isn't a single one who hasn't been thoroughly investigated,' Morely assured him, 'there isn't one whose record hasn't been irreproachable, staff and members alike. There's been no hint of suspicion against any one of them until you had your visit from Simon, and gave your story against him. I wouldn't like to guarantee that you're right to suspect him. You might be, but there isn't a blemish on his record, and the fact that Cranton has often used him for undercover work isn't exactly against him.'

'No,' said Dawlish. 'Oroshu, now. He's a Jap.'

'English-born, English-bred, went to Tokio for about six years but came back because he couldn't stand it,' said Morely.

Dawlish nodded, still keeping to himself the details of his misadventure at the Aliens' Club.

'The next thing, then. Did you get any of the men from Portiman Square?'

'We picked up the machine-gunner,' said Morely. 'He was dead—suicide. There was the other fellow in the dining-room, an American with a bad reputation, but he won't talk, or he hasn't done yet. All the rest got away.'

'Hmm,' murmured Dawlish. 'All of them Japs, from what I could see.'

'You only saw a few of them,' said Morely. 'There was a goodly proportion of Europeans.'

'It looks to me as if they had been to another Conference,' Dawlish mused, and explained what North and Georgette had told him. 'I think, Archie, that it could explain a lot. The connection between economics and the War office, for instance. I don't think a single move in this affair has gone as Cranton planned it. I think that the fact which Wilson discovered and passed on to Breddon and Cranton was a very simple one, and itself explains the great hush-hush. I think,' went on Dawlish more quickly, 'that there was just one mistake made in the first place. Someone whom they thought they could trust knew about Cranton, and the instructions to me, and worked too swiftly for any of us.'

'For heaven's sake, no riddles,' said Morely sourly. 'There isn't time for them.'

Dawlish said: 'All right, then here it is. Wilson held his Conferences from time to time and discovered that under their cover spy-stuff was being handled. He didn't want to believe it. But he made his own little investigations, and this worried the other side, so they warned him to retire or give the game up. He didn't. He told Breddon, who saw it as a Secret Service job, and saw Cranton or Chumley, it doesn't matter who he really told first. Do you follow me?'

'Follow you!' exclaimed Morely, jumping to his feet. 'I'm right behind you, Pat!'

'It's only what we should have known from the first,' said Dawlish deprecatingly. 'Cranton wanted me to work against the Conference, planned to keep everything hushed and secret, so that there could be no suspicion of investigation. Hence the approach to me, instead of to you.'

He stopped, while Morely looked at him with enthusiastic expectation.

Dawlish felt that he was beginning to see through the maze at last. The trouble centred on Wilson's Conferences, and one such Conference had been held that day, only to be broken up. He did not doubt that there would be other meeting places. As for Simon, Oroshu, North and Georgette, he was as much at sea as ever. He saw only the outline of the thing; he did not know the real motive, he did not know what the Conference planned to do.

Had Cranton or Wilson known that?

He doubted it; he believed that his task was to have been the discovering of the real *modus operandi* of the organisation, and its real purpose. He did not think that he was any nearer that, than he had been when he had first heard that Cranton wanted him on the telephone; but he did believe the decks were cleared for action, and he saw one course standing waiting for him.

He felt keyed up, impatient, eager. He wanted everything done at once, yet had to be sure that nothing was done precipitously. His mind was racing at high speed and he was oblivious to Morely's presence, even to Felicity in the next room, when the front door bell rang sharply.

CHAPTER SEVENTEEN

UNLAWFUL ENTRY

The ringing of the bell broke his mood of triumph, and Dawlish rose to his feet. When he opened the door he saw a dumpy little woman in nurse's uniform.

'Good evening, sir, Dr. Miller has given me instructions that my patient must not be moved. Please take me to her.'

A round red face beamed at him as the woman bustled through into the bedroom with an air of importance and efficiency.

Dawlish watched the door close, and turned to Morely.

'Munk's waiting for you, isn't he?'

'He should be.'

'Can you spare him for the night?'

'Yes, if you want him. What——'

'Hush!' Dawlish put a finger to his lips. 'Action we said, Archie, and we start before we realise it!'

Morely looked at him, puzzled by the change in his manner and his strange intentness.

'Archie, she's a fake. I rang for the nurse, Miller didn't. The Home that sent her didn't know what doctor was in attendance, I just asked for a night nurse. How does this one know so much?'

Morely said: 'Well I'm damned!'

'We all will be if we're not careful,' said Dawlish. He laid a hand on Morely's arm as he led the A.C. to the front door. 'I'm taking a chance that they've planted her here to report on my comings and goings. If they'd wanted to kill Felicity they wouldn't have spared the first dose. Clever, really.'

'You mean——' began Morely.

'Yes, of course that's what I mean. They caught Felicity and doped her, knowing she would need a nurse, they had the flat watched and chose their moment perfectly. Let's admit it's clever. But it's also another mistake, that's why I want Munk,' he added, opening the front door. 'He can stay here until I'm back. He should be capable of staying around without letting his presence be known.'

Morely said: 'I'll get him.'

'You stay here, I'll talk to him,' said Dawlish firmly.

Munk was a shadow in the blackout. As Dawlish neared, a muttered stream of uncomplimentary adjectives greeted him. Dawlish did not know of another policeman who expressed himself so freely when out of the A.C.'s presence.

'There's a job for you,' Dawlish whispered, 'and only you can do it well.'

Munk was mollified.

'There's a nurse in my flat, looking after Miss Deverall,' Dawlish told him. 'She, the nurse, wants watching. I'm going out, and she'll think the flat's empty. It won't be, because you'll be there.'

Munk grunted. 'Who do you think I am, the invisible man?'

'Yes,' said Dawlish. 'I'll be away for about two hours.'

'Okay, okay,' said Munk, 'she won't 'ear me breave.'

Upstairs Morely did no more than nod to the sergeant, who slipped silently into the room. Dawlish picked up his hat and cane, found his gloves and called:

'I'll be back as soon as I can, nurse.'

'Yes, sir, that's all right, sir.'

Dawlish closed the door firmly, and joined Morely on the landing.

'And where are you going now?'

'For a walk,' said Dawlish cryptically, and then laughed. 'Sorry, Archie, but I feel mysterious. I've seen so many things in the last hour, and I'm taking a lot of chances. Bear with me. When's Trivett coming out of hospital, by the way?'

'In the morning,' said Morely 'I wish you'd tell me where you're going.'

'I will, when I'm back,' said Dawlish. 'Meanwhile the call is for Simon J. Simon. We want him in, and we want him quickly, for questioning.'

'We'll find him,' said Morely grimly.

He did not hide the fact that he was dissatisfied when he left Dawlish, who walked for some hundred yards and then hailed a taxi. He directed the driver to take him to 31 Portiman Square, reaching the house ten minutes later.

He paid the driver off and approached the front door.

He tried the handle, finding that the door would not move. He had not expected it to. He turned to the window on the right, examining it briefly, to find out whether it was open.

It was not.

The faint light from the 'stars' which had replaced the arc lights in the Square was enough to enable him to see what he was doing, although not enough for him to be seen, at a casual glance, by any passerby.

He left the window and tried the one on the other side. That also was closed. He went back to the porch, examined the supporting pillars, and found he could haul himself up to the flat roof with little difficulty. That done, he explored the nearer window, finding that it was open a few inches at the top. It was one of the old sash-cord type, and needed little pressure to push it wider open. Carefully he climbed through into the room beyond.

It was very dark, and he waited for some seconds to accustom himself to the gloom. Even then it was impossible to distinguish the objects in the room, although he could just see a streak of light beneath the door. He approached it, and stepped into a passage.

A faint light was coming from a lamp burning in the hall below. He closed the bedroom door and crept towards the

110

landing, ears alert for the slightest sound; but there was utter silence in 31 Portiman Square. Glancing over the balustrade he saw the empty hall, nodded with satisfaction, and then reconstructed his approach to the landing earlier in the day. Thus he was able to judge which was Georgette's room.

He approached it cautiously. Only darkness greeted him when he opened the door and stepped inside. He took a torch from his pocket and shone its beam about the room. It lit up the ghostly outline of the four-poster bed. It was empty.

He left the room and went softly down the carpeted staircase. A murmur of voices from one of the reception rooms reached his ears, and he approached the door from which it was coming. A girl's voice alternated with a man's. Georgette's and North's.

The key was in the outside of the door.

He turned it softly. The lock made no sound, nor was there any when he withdrew the key and dropped it into his pocket. Satisfied, he went back to the first floor, looking in every room he passed until he found a study. He stepped inside, closed the door, and switched on the light.

Everything was neat and orderly, and he was reminded of Chumley's study at Chelsea. He went to the large, flat-topped desk, finding it locked; he forced the lock with a penknife, a task which took him five minutes, and then opened the middle drawer; the other drawers opened without further trouble.

Quickly he ran through the papers he found.

There were long, tedious letters on economic problems, there was correspondence with a large number of people mostly so abstruse and involved that Dawlish did not try to understand them. He worked quickly, going through file after file, until he found a loose-leaf book of quarto-size. Opening it, he found that it was an address book; and opposite each name and address there was a series of dates.

He pored over it for five minutes, nodding approvingly once or twice, for against many of the names was that day's date—April 17th. From this Dawlish inferred that the men concerned had been called to the Conference he had helped to disturb.

Writing quickly, he made a list of the names and addresses;

there were twenty-seven, so the police had been two out. Simon was not amongst them, although his name was in the book; his address given as the Aliens' Club.

Dawlish closed the book and replaced it. When the desk was opened again the fact that it had been forced would be obvious, but he did not think that was of great importance. Finished, he went out of the study and then hurried down the stairs. Only North's voice was audible, and that was drowned suddenly when the wireless was switched on and chamber music filled the room beyond.

Dawlish unlocked the door but did not open it, then went along the hall and out of the house through the front door. He stood on the porch with both hands in his pockets, surveying the faintly-lighted Square, remembering the scene there earlier in the day.

He turned again, and as if he had just arrived, rang the bell. There was no immediate answer, no sign that he had been heard, and nothing sounded from the hall until he had thundered on the knocker. Then a faint light showed beyond the glass-panelled door, and North eventually opened it.

'Yes?' He spoke sharply.

'I've been ringing and knocking for ten minutes,' said Dawlish complainingly, 'where are your servants?'

'You ought to know,' grumbled North. 'Grey was arrested this evening. He——' North stopping abruptly. 'Well, what do you want?'

'More information,' said Dawlish abruptly, and led the way to the room from which light was shining.

North shrugged his shoulders, with a resigned glance towards Georgette.

'It's our fairy godfather again,' he said.

Dawlish smiled briefly.

'Very funny. I hope my next remark will seem as humorous. I've just heard that the police have decided that on the evidence you'll both be safer in jail.'

Georgette's body stiffened.

North swore, but did not move.

The silence in the room was emphasised by the heavy breathing of both the man and the girl. Not until some seconds afterwards did Georgette say in a tense voice:

'Why?'

Dawlish shrugged.

'They have the evidence,' he said. 'It may have been planted on you. I think it was. But I can't hold them back any longer.'

'I don't believe you've tried!' snapped North.

'Why should he try?' asked Georgette slowly. 'It's inevitable, I've felt that almost from the first. Everything's against us, Gerry, everything's worked the wrong way.'

North said furiously: 'It's so damnably unfair! We've done nothing, nothing at all!'

'The police don't usually get convictions when the accused is innocent,' Dawlish said equably. 'Well, there it is. I wish I could help you more.'

He half-turned, but North blocked his way to the door, saying sharply:

'Why did you come to warn us?'

Dawlish frowned. 'Fair's fair, when all's said and done.'

'I don't believe it! More likely you persuaded them to do this. I've an idea that you've been double-crossing us from the start!'

'Don't get hysterical,' said Dawlish with distaste.

He pushed North aside, and walked along the hall. Silence fell behind him, broken suddenly by North's hurried feet.

'Dawlish! Dawlish! When are they coming?'

'I don't know, not having second sight,' answered Dawlish, 'but they're not usually a long time. I think——' He paused, and then went on: 'Who are you most worried about, North? Yourself, or Georgette?'

North snapped: 'Georgette, of course. Damn it, Dawlish, I'm not a fool. We've been talking about it since we got back. The evidence is strongly against her, and I'd give a fortune to have the chance to prove that it's wrong. Can't you do *any*thing to get us a respite?'

There was another period of silence, and then Dawlish said quietly:

'I've some friends who would probably look after Georgette for a few days, and no one need know anything about it.'

'No, we'll both keep together,' said Georgette quickly.

North rounded on her.

'Don't be stubborn, darling, it's a chance in a thousand.' His voice was eager. 'Will you do that, Dawlish? I don't believe they'll ever prove the case against Georgette, but I know what it will be like. Question after question, browbeating and insults. And just now—hasn't she got enough on her mind? Isn't it damnable enough?'

'Yes,' said Dawlish slowly. 'Well, I can try to help her, North, but you——'

'I'll be all right,' North said briskly. 'Don't worry about me. When can she start?'

'As soon as she puts her coat on,' said Dawlish.

Georgette was dubious, but North urged her to agree. In five minutes she was ready. North hurried them to the door, breathing his thanks. He would never forget it, never.

The door closed on Dawlish and Georgette.

'Are you sure——' Georgette began.

'I'm quite sure,' said Dawlish, tucking her arm in his. 'Don't worry, Georgette, there'll be plenty to worry about as you get older.'

Walking quickly they reached the end of the Square, then turned the corner which led to Oxford Street. The headlights of a car flashed suddenly on their backs.

Georgette started.

At the same moment Dawlish flung her forward. As he did so something dropped not ten yards behind them. There was a pause followed by a brilliant flash of light which made even the glare of the headlamps seem dim. Fast upon it came the roar of an explosion. The blast hurled both of them flat against the wall of a house.

The roar had deafened them, the light had blinded them, while round them bricks and mortar tumbled to the long, rumbling sound which had been so familiar in London during the blitz. Before it had stopped footsteps sounded, although neither Dawlish nor Georgette could hear them.

Steel-hatted wardens in A.R.P. overalls bent over the couple and helped them to their feet.

While they were doing so there came another flash.

It took all of them by surprise, including Dawlish. He saw the flash and covered his ears against the explosion. The roar before had been trivial compared with this one. The very ground shook as if from an earthquake.

Dawlish felt Georgette's hand leap unsteadily on his arm. He looked down at her face, lighted by the lurid glare. She had recovered quickly and well from the first shock, and he admired her steadiness as she said:

'Where was that?'

'We'll go and see,' said Dawlish.

As they turned back, the glare from the fire, which had started, lit up every corner of the Square. It revealed the people who had defied precautions and rushed out to see whether they could help. Flames leapt hundreds of feet into the air, not from a house but from the shell of one, and the ruins of two others on either side.

The shell had been Number 31.

CHAPTER EIGHTEEN

TIDINGS FROM TED

Georgette's hand no longer trembled, but Dawlish felt her fingers biting into his arm. He watched the conflagration for several seconds, then slowly turned away. The crowd which had gathered was being advised by wardens to get to the shelters; few doubted that the explosion had been caused by a bomb.

'Can you make it?' Dawlish asked, as Georgette turned stiffly.

'Yes.' He just heard the word. 'I—no. We can't go. Gerry was in there, Gerry stayed back. Oh my God!'

Dawlish said: 'There's nothing we can do to help, Georgette. Remember, he wanted you to get away as soon as you could.'

She was taking in deep breaths of air as he made her walk, sobs shaking her akin to those she had released at the White Hart, in Salisbury. He urged her on, until the crowd was thin and he was able to get a taxi.

He bundled Georgette into the cab, directing the driver to Jermyn Street. The glow of firelight gradually lessened as they were carried further away, but it was still showing red in the sky when the taxi drew up outside the house.

Dawlish helped Georgette out, and paid off the cab. He opened the door of the flat with his key, making plenty of noise to warn both Munk and the nurse. The latter was standing on the threshold of the bedroom door. She bustled forward.

'Well, you haven't been long! Dearie me, I thought you would be out all the evening. Did you hear it?'

'What?' asked Dawlish.

'Why, the bomb. And no *warning*. I think it's shameful if they can't even sound a *warn*ing when those devils come over. What is the government coming to?' Curiosity overwhelmed her at last. 'Is there anything the matter, sir? Can I make a cup of tea or anything?'

'Yes, please,' said Dawlish. 'A strong one.'

Georgette sat down. Animation, even life itself, seemed to have gone out of her. Dawlish went into the small spare bedroom; as he expected Munk was standing behind the door.

Munk made wild signs, enjoining silence, while taking a notebook from his pocket and tearing out two pages which he thrust into Dawlish's hand. Dawlish slipped them into his pocket, and whispered:

'Stay a bit longer, will you?'

Munk, pretending annoyance, was actually pleased. Sure of this, Dawlish rejoined Georgette. He helped her to drink a cup of tea, while the nurse stood watching her curiously. Dawlish went into the bathroom and ran water into the hand basin while reading Munk's note.

It read:

Telephoned 9.51 p.m. Number unknown. Said Lucy was okay, nothing special to report, Dawlish had gone out leav-

116

ing her alone. Closed down. Telephone rang 10.11 p.m. Nurse said Lucy speaking, no Dawlish did not seem to suspect anything, Lucy did not know where he had gone. Promised to try to find out, goodbye.

Dialled for the number, therefore presume it is in the London area, impossible for me to see what number she was calling.

Nurse appeared happy, humming to herself, doing some knitting. Talked affectionately to her patient.

Dawlish re read it, nodded as if with satisfaction, and returned the note to his pocket; Munk was doing well.

When Dawlish returned to the lounge the nurse was by the bedroom door. She looked back with a smile, saying:

'You couldn't have gone far, sir, coming back as soon as that. Did you have an accident, or something?' She looked towards Georgette, patently fishing.

Dawlish said gravely: 'No, not what you'd call one, nurse. How is your patient?'

'Oh, she'll be all right before long. I don't think you need worry about her, sir, but I always say that it's as well to have someone near who knows what to do in an emergency. Dear me! It's that front door again. I hope the ring won't disturb my patient. Shall I open it?'

'Thanks, I'll go,' said Dawlish.

A loud voice was demanding something better in the way of service, and Dawlish's smile was spontaneous and warm as he admitted Ted Beresford. Ted declared on sight of his friend that he was not used to being kept waiting, and it had come as a shock to him. He screwed up his ugly face in an expression of mock displeasure, but his eyes were gleaming, and there was an atmosphere of expectancy about him.

His voice, however, was offhand as he drawled: 'Anything happening?'

'Many things,' said Dawlish, signalling for caution. The nurse was a problem, and he was uncertain whether it would be wise to let her know that he realised what she was doing. There was no doubt, however, that from a nursing point of view, Felicity was receiving competent treatment.

That lined up with one other incident, and only one: it was a method of working similar to Oroshu's. Felicity had been knocked out and drugged, but not seriously harmed. It had been done simply as a means of inveigling Lucy into the flat, just as when Dawlish had been shanghaied at the Aliens' Club it had been solely to keep him out of action for a couple of hours.

Quick to take the hint, Ted's eyes roamed the lounge. 'Trouble?'

'Plenty, but it could be worse.' Dawlish felt on safe ground here, even with Lucy listening. He explained what had happened to Tim and then to Felicity, and he made a strong point of his suspicions of Simon J. Simon.

'We don't know where he is,' Dawlish went on. 'There are so many things we don't know, Ted. For instance, why was an attempt made to kill me and Georgette when we left 31 Portiman Square, and why was it blown up soon after we'd gone?'

Beresford's face was a study in astonishment.

'Good Lord! Heavy work, Pat. What's the trouble? Got them on the run, d'you think?'

'I'm hoping so,' said Dawlish. 'They should be getting worried by now. And what have *you* got to report?'

Beresford said: 'And how the devil d'you know there's anything *to* report?'

'Don't pretend, old boy,' Dawlish exhorted him. 'You're keeping it up your sleeve and waiting for the surprise effect. What is it?'

'Does it show that much?'

'It does indeed. What's doing?'

'Well, about Goo-goo and her rheumatic spouse,' said Beresford, launching forth with obvious pleasure, 'I began to wonder whether they were following me or I was following them. They left the Royal just before I left my pub, in—believe me or not—a chauffeur-driven car heading for London. I heard her tell the chauffeur to make for London, but Freddie and Hermina are on their tail. Missed dinner, and Freddie will curse, but he'll get over it. So we're all in the old metropolis, Pat, or pretty close to it. Not bad, eh?'

118

Dawlish agreed that it was not bad, but maintained that it was not necessarily good. He wished that Beresford had followed the Mooneys himself, but admitted that he had done what appeared to be the right thing by hurrying to the flat.

Beresford did not know that he had been summoned solely because Dawlish felt that he needed some support other than the police. Dawlish broke that news gently, and Beresford scowled.

'And I thought you had a special spot of bother for me, drat you. Any idea what it's all about?'

'None at all,' lied Dawlish, thinking of Lucy. 'Did you say you'd missed dinner?'

'I did.'

'We'll go out for a snack,' Dawlish said, 'but we don't want to be long in case Freddie rings up.'

'Freddie won't, Hermina wears the trousers. Nice woman that,' declared Beresford, 'but I wouldn't like to live with her, she's too high-powered for a comfortable life. Shouldn't be surprised if Freddie stays in the army.' He stumbled purposely over the mat on the landing, whispering under cover of this: 'What's under your skin? Why the hush-hush in the flat?'

Dawlish, his low voice hidden beneath the loud exclamations of disaster, whispered back: .

'The nurse has been planted by the opposition. Munk's holding a watching brief, and I'm hoping he'll get information worth having while we're out. But we mustn't be too long.'

They found a snack bar which provided them with sandwiches and coffee, which they readily consumed while Dawlish outlined what had happened and what he had done. It was the first time for a long while that he had been able to talk freely to anyone, Felicity excepted; and even to her there had been one or two things he had thought it wiser to keep to himself.

Beresford nodded and ate, ate and nodded, and passed no comment until Dawlish finished. Then the large man screwed up his face and appeared to study a cherubim painted on the wall by an artist with an unsteady hand but a nice eye for figure work.

'You've been pretty scatterbrained, old son. Not like you. Or are you keeping the real stuff back?'

'Some conclusions yes, but no incidents.'

'The incidents are all right,' declared Beresford, 'it's what you haven't done that worries me. This Arthurson cove, for instance, and the other secretary, Fuelling.'

'The police are watching them.'

'Um, yes. Oroshu?'

'The police give him a reputation second to none.'

Beresford closed one eye, then opened it again abruptly as the maid behind the snack bar winked back and made towards him. He engaged her in a few seconds of skittish conversation until another customer claimed her attention, and then returned to Dawlish aggrievedly.

'Why did that have to happen? It's interrupted my train of thought. What was I going to say?'

'Probably comment on my loyalty to the police and their opinions,' said Dawlish.

Beresford grinned. 'And so I was. They don't seem to have shone so far.'

'No one's been shining,' said Dawlish, 'unless it's Simon and Company, and I'm not so sure about them. What I did forget to tell you,' he added, 'is about North and Georgette.' He explained his visit to Portiman Square, and his decision to throw another scare into the couple.

Beresford's eyes grew sombre as Dawlish reached the end, and after a pause he said:

'Things happen that way to you, don't they? You do a thing for no reason at all, and as a result of it the girl just misses death by a yard or so.'

'You can hardly say "for no reason at all",' exhorted Dawlish. 'I wanted them scared, I wanted to see what they would do when they believed the police were about to use the handcuffs. Incidentally, why limit death to Georgette?'

'Well,' said Beresford, 'I rather wondered whether North did, in fact, stay behind. I mean, you'd given him plenty of reason for wanting to get moving, and I fancy that with the girl off his hands he wouldn't lose much time. He was probably as far away from Number 31 as you were. If he wasn't, he was pretty slow.'

Dawlish grunted. 'It could be, yes.'

'Of course it could,' went on Beresford, much encouraged. 'North would know he hadn't much chance of getting clear away *with* Georgette, but a man can make a fair job of hiding on his own. North didn't want Georgette about his neck. He believed her safer with you. Natural attitude, when all's said and done.'

'Objection,' murmured Dawlish. 'He expressed grave doubts of my sincerity.'

'He *said* he did,' declared Beresford heavily. 'But my bet is that North had the wind up because of the way things have gone, and wanted to try out one or two lines of his own before the police got him. They can't let him go free for long, and he must know it.'

Beresford glanced at his wrist-watch.

'Do you know that it's just on midnight?'

'As late as that! We'd better get back,' said Dawlish, 'and find what's been happening at the flat. Munk will get writer's cramp if we leave him there much longer.'

'And Hermina might ring up,' Beresford reminded him. 'Pat,' he went on, 'between ourselves I wouldn't say you were at your brightest and best.'

'I'm not,' said Dawlish. 'I caught a cold on manoeuvres. Felicity made me sweat it out, but it comes back in snatches, making it difficult to concentrate. You know the feeling.'

'Me?' asked Beresford in surprise. 'Concentrate? Certainly not, old son, I leave that to you.'

They reached the house after two minutes of sharp walking, and were in the hall when a shout came from upstairs.

It was a woman's voice, followed by an unmistakable oath in Munk's harsh tones. The oath was followed by a thud, and then a door opened and light streamed on to the landing.

'Porch!' hissed Dawlish.

He withdrew swiftly with Beresford close behind him. They waited on either side of the porch while the nurse rushed downstairs. She was running wildly, her heels clattering on the stairs. There was no sound of pursuit, but Munk's voice roared:

'Help! Police! Stop her!'

As Lucy reached the porch, Dawlish and Beresford dropped

121

their arms about her. She was caught without a chance of getting away, and so flabbergasted that for a moment she did not even try. Beresford saw her furious face, and murmured:

'Oranges and Lemons, the bells of St. Clement's, *out*!'

Lucy kicked him viciously on the shin.

'Ouch!' exclaimed Beresford but tightened his grip. 'I'll remember that against you, vixen. Got her, Pat?'

'You carry her up,' said Dawlish.

The nurse was plump, and by now extremely active, but Beresford's strength and length of arm had no difficulty at all in imprisoning her.

They found Munk sitting in the middle of the lounge nursing his right ankle. He glared up at the nurse with utmost ferocity.

'She's broken my ankle!' he snarled.

'I've an idea,' said Beresford, 'that she's broken my shin.'

'Well, what happened?' Dawlish asked briskly.

'The phone rang, Mr. Dawlish, an' I opened the door to git a better look at 'er,' Munk volunteered. 'She answered it and said you was out, and then looked over 'er shoulder, and saw me. She jumped for that door quicker'n you can say "knife", hurling a chair at me on the way. Took it on the ankle, and the ruddy bone's broken, or something.'

Dawlish helped him to the settee, while Beresford dumped Lucy on an easy chair. She had quietened considerably, but there was no love in her brown eyes.

'Well, so what?' she snapped.

'That's the question,' said Dawlish, 'and you'll know the answer when we find the woman you impersonated. If she's hurt I wouldn't like to be in your shoes, my sweet. Did she phone anyone else, Munk?'

'Sure she did,' said Munk, with aggressive satisfaction. 'Wasn't so careful this time, neither. Mr. Simon, she asked for, at the Aliens' Club. *And* she spoke to 'im.'

'So Simon sent her!' exclaimed Dawlish. 'We're certainly getting on.' He stepped towards the telephone but before he lifted it the bell rang. 'Dawlish speaking,' he said into the mouthpiece, and was almost deafened by a distorted voice which blared incoherently. Dawlish stemmed the flood at last.

'It's Hermina!' shrieked the voice on a slightly lower key. 'I've just hurried away from Freddie for a minute to telephone!'

'Where are you?' Dawlish demanded. 'Where have they gone?'

'Who? Oh, them! That's what I was going to tell you, if you'd only listen. Freddie says it's the Foreigners' Club ... oh, the Aliens' Club ... Well, it's the same thing, really, isn't it ... speak up, I can't hear you ... yes, of course, both of them went in, about ten minutes ago. What? ... oh, all right, we'll wait, but don't keep us long, Freddie's hungry.'

Hermina rang off.

Dawlish turned quickly from the telephone, but kept his finger on the bridge.

'The Mooneys have gone to the Club, too. We'll get them with Simon if we can move fast enough.' He released the bridge and dialled Whitehall. 'Hello, Scotland Yard ... is Sir Archibald Morely there, please? ... Yes, I'll hold on.' He paused, looking at the nurse, whose eyes glared vindictively, and then he heard Morely's voice over the wire.

Morely listened, said little, but promised to have the Club surrounded within twenty minutes.

CHAPTER NINETEEN

'MR. SIMON HAS LEFT'

It proved that a plain-clothes man, on duty outside 88g Jermyn Street, called to inquire about the shouting and the possibility that help was needed. He solved a problem, for Dawlish left him at the flat with the nurse, Georgette, and Munk. Dawlish told the plain-clothes man to ring for more help, and with Beresford hurried down the stairs.

Although it was nearly half-past twelve a taxi appeared before they had gone fifty yards, and they were at the Aliens' Club within ten minutes of leaving the flat.

With the departure of the cab Dawlish and Beresford found themselves in utter darkness, and alone. But not for long, however. Out of the gloom materialised a man in a light mackintosh.

'Is that you, Dawlish?'

'Hallo, Archie! Quick work!' Dawlish was genuinely relieved to find Morely already present. 'How are things moving?'

'We'll be ready in five minutes.'

'Good. Simon shouldn't have taken fright yet. Had you tried the Club for him?'

'Oroshu swore that he wasn't here,' said Morely. 'I'll have a word with Oroshu before the night's out.'

'And Oroshu will consign honourable policeman to land of beautiful fire and brimstone,' suggested Dawlish. 'Five minutes, you said?'

'Don't be impatient,' said Morely. 'We don't want to start in too soon.'

Dawlish waited for another two minutes, and then a shrouded figure approached to report that the Club was surrounded. Morely uttered his satisfaction, while Dawlish gripped his right arm and Beresford's left. Thus the trio went up the steps and into the foyer of the Aliens' Club.

A little olive-skinned man with a fez and white gloves bowed his way towards them.

'Mr. Simon, please,' said Morely.

'Pardon, sir? But Mr. Simon is not 'ere. Three-four gentlemen attempt to see him. Regrets, gentlemen.'

'I'll see Mr. Oroshu,' said Morely quietly.

'Okay.' The porter retired to his glass screened cubby hole. Into the telephone he fired a gabble of words, and then rounded the screen again.

'One-two minutes waiting, please, no more.' He bowed.

A voice spoke from behind him, flat, imperturbable.

'Good evening, sir. I am Oroshu, the manager. At your service, I need not say.'

'Ah.' Morely spoke quickly. 'A Mr. Simon is staying here. I

want to see him at once.'

'Your pardon, sir. Mr. Simon has not been here since lunch-time. There have been many inquiries for him.'

Morely said : 'I am the Assistant Commissioner of Police, and I have information that Simon is here. The Club will be searched unless you take me to him immediately.'

'It is regrettable,' Oroshu said blandly. 'He reserved no room, he is not here tonight. You have been badly informed, Mr. Assistant Commissioner.' He bowed.

'You have five minutes to change your mind.' Dawlish imagined that Morely was restraining his temper with an effort. 'Another matter, Oroshu. A lady and gentleman, calling themselves Mr. and Mrs. Felix Mooney, arrived here about three-quarters of an hour ago.'

'Mr. and Mrs. Mooney, yes,' Oroshu said. 'You wish to see them?'

'After we've seen Simon.'

Oroshu shrugged.

'You wish to have your men search the Club?'

'Yes,' said Morely, and on his words two plain-clothes men entered. 'Get four more men, Dobson,' Morely instructed. 'You know the man you're looking for?'

'Yes, sir.'

'It is not out of place for me to advise you that you will be disturbing many of our guests and residents,' Oroshu said with dignity. 'I would like the opportunity of having them called.'

'We'll call them,' Morely said briefly. 'I'd like you to take me and Mr. Dawlish to the Mooneys' room.'

'I am at your command.' Another stiff bow, as, with more flat-footed dignity, Oroshu led the way to the stairs.

At the top of them was a wide passage, doors plainly num-bered on either side.

'Number 11, please,' Oroshu said, and tapped.

There was no answer, and he tapped again, then attempted, unsuccessfully, to open the door. Morely tightened his lips, but Oroshu anticipated his request. 'I will send for the master-key, Mr. Assistant Commissioner.' He pressed a bell, and a maid appeared very quickly. 'Open this door, please,' Oroshu said.

The maid, dusky-skinned and large-bosomed, inserted a key

which dangled from a belt at her waist, and turned it in the lock. She pushed the door open, and Oroshu stood aside for the others to enter.

Morely went first, Dawlish close on his heels. He was so close that when Morely stopped abruptly Dawlish cannoned into him.

Morely's exclamation was not wholly because of the collision.

The woman and her husband were lying in chairs close to each other. In the man's hand there was an automatic. A bullet had entered the woman's forehead, drilling a small, neat hole from which blood still trickled. A similar wound, although larger and more ugly, was in the side of the man's head.

It was quite useless to ask questions, impossible to expect any man to assume that there was more to the double killing than met the eye. Mooney's prints were on the gun, and the gun declared that Mooney had shot the woman and then himself.

After some time, when the police experts had finished their work, Dawlish murmured:

'The verdict will be jealousy, of course. A more perfect motive couldn't be found for them. Husband's jealousy of wife's devotion to men in uniform. Eh, Ted?'

Beresford nodded.

From across a table in Oroshu's office, Morely regarded them without pleasure.

'No sign at all of Simon, Pat. Are you sure that you haven't been trying to get us into action by faking a statement?'

Dawlish said sharply: 'Certainly not. Munk gave me the information. It's above question. The nurse telephoned Simon here. Or,' he added under his breath, 'she made it appear that she did.'

'What's that?' snapped Morely.

'Just a remark,' said Dawlish evenly. 'Look, we don't have to get worked up about it. The evidence says that Simon was telephoned here, and actually talked to the nurse. On that basis, Oroshu isn't telling the truth.'

From the fireplace the Japanese said: 'May I suggest, Mr.

Dawlish, that there is difficulty enough here without the further complication of suspecting me of lying? I have no purpose in doing so.' He paused. 'What do you propose now, Mr. Assistant Commissioner?'

Morely looked at him coldly; Dawlish had rarely seen the A.C. so uncompromisingly hostile.

'The Club will be under police guard until morning, when a further inquiry will be held. Meanwhile, no one leaves without the express permission of the police.'

'If it is your wish,' Oroshu said between his teeth.

'It's my instruction,' Morely rejoined tartly.

With Dawlish and Beresford he was outside five minutes later, climbing into his car. He promised to run the others to Jermyn Street, but was silent on the way.

Dawlish suggested that he joined them in a drink, and after some hesitation Morely accepted. But he remained silent until Dawlish had poured three whiskies-and-sodas.

Beresford could contain himself no longer.

'Demonstration of ruthless behaviour of police noted,' he said, raising his glass. 'Why so dour, Archie?'

'Dour?' Morely laughed shortly. 'I believe that little swine smuggled Simon out before we got there, or after we arrived. I want Simon badly,' he added, and when Dawlish regarded him curiously he added: 'Simon visited the War Office this evening, got to Cranton's office, and got away with several papers of importance. McKyc contacted the Home Secretary and there's been the devil to pay.'

'Well, well!' exclaimed Beresford. 'What happened? Did they show him round, with apologies for taking so long about it?'

'Don't play the fool,' Morely said irritably. 'He's often been to Cranton's office, and the officials weren't advised that we wanted him in. It was barefaced effrontery, and he got away with it. I thought we had him when you phoned, Pat.'

Dawlish rubbed the side of his nose.

'Ill-temper well understood,' he acknowledged. 'But at least things are moving.' He went into details about the developments at Portiman Square, and Morely said that for safety's sake he would put out a general call for North.

127

'But the explosion may have been to get rid of North and the girl,' he said. 'In much the same way that the Mooneys were murdered. You were lucky to get away when you did.'

'Yes,' admitted Dawlish, and then gave an exclamation of annoyance. 'Good Lord, I've left Freddie and Hermina cooling their heels near the Aliens' Club. Talking of the devil to pay, this will beat it! Ted——'

'All right, I'll go,' Ted forestalled him disgustedly.

'I'll come downstairs with you,' Morely said. 'There's no point in staying longer.'

Dawlish was left alone with the knowledge that the two plain-clothes men would remain on duty outside.

Georgette was no different from when he had last seen her, sleeping heavily and tossing and turning as if her sleep was troubled. For safety's sake he turned the key in the lock of her door, and then went into Felicity. He stayed there for some time, until he was disturbed by a knock at the front door. It proved to be Miller, who apologised gruffly and explained that he had been called out on an urgent case. He looked even more tired than earlier in the day, and after a brief examination declared that Felicity was getting on well. He was not in the flat for more than five minutes.

Ted Beresford was away for twenty, and to Dawlish's relief returned alone. He had persuaded the Blakes to go to their London flat, saying that Dawlish was out and would not be back that night.

Dawlish smiled faintly.

'Thanks, Ted.' He yawned, and settled back in his chair. 'Both beds being occupied we'd better make shift here for the night.'

Lazily they dragged chairs and blankets into position, and settled down to sleep as best they could. Beresford dropped off within ten minutes, but Dawlish was a long time in the halfway stage between sleeping and waking. He slept at last, and there was no sound in the flat except for Beresford's faint snoring and the creak of a chair as Dawlish turned over.

There was no suggestion of fatigue about Mr. Simon J. Simon when that swarthy gentlemam, in pyjamas and dressing-

128

gown, sat at ease in a London flat not half a mile from Jermyn Street. In front of him were several papers each of which, when read, he put aside with a nod of satisfaction.

Occasionally he sipped a weak whisky-and-soda at his side.

It was three o'clock when he finished, but he did not go immediately to bed. Instead he lifted a telephone, and dialled a Chelsea number. There was a long pause before a gruff voice answered.

'Who's that?'

'Simon, my friend,' said Simon gently. 'I am sorry to disturb you so late, but I want a complete summary of what has happened today, and I need it by six o'clock. Do you think you can manage to obtain it, Fuelling?'

'Six o'clock,' Fuelling grunted. 'It doesn't leave much time.'

'Time enough for a young man like you,' chided Simon. 'All the incidents, please, and all the reports. I expect you to work for me as earnestly as you would have worked for the Professor.'

'Oh heck,' said Fuelling. 'I'll get the report out.'

'Good. Have you had any word from Arthurson?'

'No.'

'If he should telephone you, refer him to me immediately.'

Simon was smiling when he replaced the receiver. He continued to do so as, deep in thought, he folded his hands across his ample stomach. Finally he stood up, saying audibly:

'Dawlish can wait until morning, I think. He will need a little sleep.' He chuckled as if the joke amused him, then took off his dressing-gown, kicked off his slippers and climbed into bed.

He was sleeping when there was a slight noise at the window of the lounge, next to his bedroom.

The curtains at the window billowed inwards. After a pause, a man's foot appeared, then his leg. There was another pause before a man climbed into the room, and then slowly approached Simon's bedroom.

In the newcomer's hand was an automatic, with the ugly snout of a silencer fitted to the barrel.

CHAPTER TWENTY

UP AND DOING

Over the face of the intruder was a dark handkerchief, drawn tautly across his cheeks and nose. A hat was pulled well down over his forehead, so that only his eyes—and those indistinctly—showed when he switched on the light.

Without hesitation he approached Simon's door. Holding the automatic firmly in his right hand he turned the handle with his left. A faint creak followed as the door opened, and he kept quite still.

Heavy breathing greeted him.

The intruder slowly trained his gun, as slowly relinquished his grip on the door handle, and went closer to the sleeping man. He took each step carefully, balancing himself before taking a second.

Suddenly Simon rolled over.

The intruder stopped abruptly, lost his head, and fired twice into the bed.

The noise from each shot was trivial, no louder than a faint sneeze.

By then another door in the flat had opened, and footsteps thudded towards the bedroom. The intruder turned and ran back to the lounge, raised his gun hand and smashed the electric bulb. A man cursed at the sudden darkness while the intruder found his way to the window, pulled aside the curtains, and climbed unsteadily out.

' 'Arf a mo',' said a rough voice, and there followed a stab of flame from the opposite side of the lounge. It revealed a large fellow wrapped in a gaudy dressing-gown, and also allowed him to glimpse the gunman then more than halfway through the window. The latter turned, sending a bullet towards the dressing-gown.

Then the gunman dropped out of sight.

Cursing, the man in the dressing-gown blundered across the room and switched on a second light.

'Put that out!' hissed Simon from the bedroom door. 'Put it out, you fool!'

There was a split second of hesitation before the other obeyed. Simon moved to the window, shut it, and pulled the curtain. Then, with a steady hand, he turned on the light. He looked sharply at his servant, seeing a patch of blood near his elbow.

He pursed his lips.

'Come into the bathroom immediately, Kennet. That will need to be dressed.'

'Okay, okay. Why didn't you let me 'ave a shot at 'im?' the man muttered. 'I couldn't've missed, he musta' bin 'arf way down the ladder.'

'The police and wardens could not have missed the light, either,' retorted Simon, stripping off Kennet's pyjama jacket and examining a flesh wound which did not look serious. He turned to a first-aid outfit. 'Your arm will be stiff for a while, but that is all. Will you never understand, Kennet, that we must not allow the police or officials to know we are here. Hasn't it sunk into your thick head yet that the slightest slip now would be fatal?' Simon's face was without fear, though he had lost most of his colour. 'That was a very narrow escape, Kennet, I had no idea that anyone knew where to find me. Except, of course, Fuelling.' He murmured the name again, then shrugged and added with a smile that held no humour: 'It would have been a very different matter, I think, had Dawlish made the visit. I cannot imagine him running quite so wildly.'

Kennet sneered.

'What, that big ape?'

'That big ape,' said Simon precisely, 'is no fool, Kennet, and no more lacks physical courage than you do. He has not had the best of assistance. He was never given a real chance, but he is sometimes disturbingly near the mark and always uncomfortably persistent.' Simon pinned a bandage into position, and there was the faintest glimmer of a smile in the dark eyes.

'Now get back to bed, and be careful not to lie on that arm. I'll have it dressed again tomorrow.'

Kennet grunted, and returned to his room. Simon spent five minutes fastidiously putting the bedclothes into order, then climbed in and, within a very few minutes, was asleep again.

At a quarter to six that morning Peter Fuelling, third secretary to Professor Wilson, pushed a heap of papers away from him and lit a cigarette. A pile of stubs over-topped the ashtray by his side. Wearily he moved through the smoke-laden room towards a small kitchenette.

'I'll bet the old devil won't want them until this afternoon,' he muttered as he ran water into a kettle. 'Just like him to make me work half the night.' He yawned, coughed, and put tea things and a tin of biscuits on a tray.

The kettle boiled, and he poured water on to the tea. There was a sharp ring at the front door bell.

'Strewth, he's here,' ejaculated Fuelling. Straightening his hair he went to the door of the two-roomed service flat.

But the caller was not Simon.

Two tall men were standing behind a shorter, thick-set one. A glaring face, an aggressive moustache, and prominent blue eyes confronted Fuelling.

'What do you want?' His voice was high-pitched and uncertain.

'Just a word with you, that's all,' growled Detective Sergeant Munk. 'In you go, Parry.' He nodded to the man behind him, who passed Fuelling quickly as the latter snapped:

'Who are you? You've no right to do this!'

'Search warrant,' declared Munk briefly. 'Want to see it?'

But Fuelling refused to look, continuing to back towards the small room where the two plain-clothes men were busy at the desk, collecting papers.

'You're Peter Augustus Fuelling?' Munk asked him, his voice suddenly official.

'Yes, I—but this is outrageous! I tell you——'

'Steady, now, steady,' said Munk. 'The less we 'ear from you the better we'll like it. And remember anything you say can be used in evidence.'

'But what are you charging me with?' demanded Fuelling, looking desperately over his shoulder. 'You can't behave like this, it's illegal!'

Munk snorted.

'*You're* a one to talk about what's illegal, I don't think. Special orders, *Mister* Fuelling, War Emergency Act, Section 19B. Want me to read it to you?'

Parry spoke with some excitement.

'I think we've got plenty here, Sergeant.'

'That's what I thought,' said Munk darkly. He was limping, but there was no slackening of his habitual ferocity. Though it was not yet daylight, the coming dawn showed faintly about the landing outside the flat.

A small, yellow-faced man crossed the threshold and was followed by another. The first Munk knew about it was a blow in the small of the back, then another across his head, both so vicious and powerful that he pitched sideways, barely conscious. Parry rushed forward, to find himself peering into the muzzle of a gun and the slanting eyes of a Japanese.

The Jap fired, and Parry fell to the ground, while the second plain-clothes man drew back against the wall, his hands flung up towards the ceiling. The Japanese gunman said nothing, while his companion collected papers from the desk and then made a hurried search through the drawers of a filing cabinet. He put everything he could find into a large briefcase, snapped its catch into position, and turned to the door.

The Jap gunman backed away.

At the last moment, Fuelling moved.

There was a heavy book on the end of the desk, and this he grabbed and threw towards the gunman. It did not reach its mark, nor spoil the Jap's aim. A second shot buried itself in Fuelling's chest. The gunman moved swiftly to the door, pausing only to tear the telephone cable from its socket. Then they went out together, leaving Munk dazed and half-conscious, Fuelling dead, Parry dying and the other plain-clothes man staring at the two bodies, temporarily so horrified that he could not think or move.

Dawlish opened his mouth in a gargantuan yawn.

Then he opened his eyes, blinked, and scowled. Slowly he stretched out his cramped legs, pulled himself to his feet and stepped unsteadily to the window.

Broad daylight swept into the room as he drew the curtains.

'Well, the weather's all right,' he muttered. Still half-asleep he stumbled into the kitchen to put on a kettle. At the sink he washed his hands and face, then, face buried in a towel, he peeped into Felicity's room.

She appeared to be sleeping normally, a slight tinge of colour tempering the heavy pallor of the previous night. He nodded with satisfaction. By then the kettle was singing, and he made tea.

Beresford was sleeping soundly, and Dawlish debated whether to wake him. But it was just after nine o'clock, and he decided that the other had slept long enough.

He gave a thump on his friend's massive shoulder.

'Come on, sluggard. Tea's made and you have to be on your way in half an hour.'

Beresford struggled to a sitting position.

'Oh damn, I'm stiff! What happened?'

'You've awakened,' said Dawlish amiably. 'Isn't that marvel enough to get on with?'

An hour later both he and Dawlish had bathed and were looking and feeling fresh and presentable. Neither of the girls had awakened, and Dawlish had decided on toast and marmalade for breakfast, rather than the rigours of cooking. He did everything in a leisurely way, not trying to force his thoughts, comfortable in the knowledge that Felicity was so much nearer normal, and further away from danger.

After breakfast his mind worked more swiftly and he contemplated the wisdom of telephoning the Yard, deciding after all that he would be wiser to wait until the Yard contacted him. In the midst of his thoughts Dr. Miller arrived.

' 'Morning, Dawlish. How is she?'

'Much improved, I think.'

'Good. I've been thinking, you shouldn't really keep her here, you know. You've too much to do, as far as I can gather. I've arranged for her to be taken to the nursing home. Is that all right with you?'

'Well,' said Dawlish, 'I suppose so. Yes, it'll be wiser.' He did not explain his hesitation by saying that he liked to think of Felicity near at hand. Second thoughts had shown him how selfish this was.

Miller came out of the bedroom rubbing his hands with satisfaction.

'Yes, she'll be all right. A day or two in bed, and she'll forget that she was ever drugged. A little bit more, though, and I doubt whether she would have come round. How's the other patient?'

'Still asleep,' said Dawlish, 'and no nursing home for her. Here she is, and here she'll stay.'

'It's up to you,' said Miller, 'but no third degree, mind.'

He bustled off, after refusing a cup of tea.

'And what now?' Beresford asked.

'It's not yet half-past ten,' Dawlish said, a trifle moodily. 'Morely's had no good news, or we would have heard of it by now. I wonder if Trivett's up and about.'

'And how Tim is,' Beresford added.

'You might ring up and find out. We don't need to wonder about the Mooneys,' Dawlish went on slowly. 'A bad show that. I'd like to know whether Oroshu had anything to do with it.'

'You aren't convinced it was murder and suicide?'

'Get that telephoning done,' said Dawlish strongly, 'and don't ask fool questions. Of course I'm not.'

Ted confirmed that Tim Jeremy was getting on well, and that it would be quite in order for a friend to visit him. He left the flat in a hurry to get Tim's story, and was back in a little more than half an hour. He reported that Tim remembered nothing except that he had kept Simon in sight, after leaving Portiman Square in the wake of Georgette and the secretary, North. He had been hit heavily over the head while in a side street, and had then staggered back to the flat.

'And before that?' inquired Dawlish. 'He told me that Georgette had led him a pretty dance.'

'Actually he tried North first,' said Beresford, 'and North, taking him for a reporter, wouldn't say anything. He hung about until North and the girl left the house after dark. He went to Chelsea, and knew that Georgette had been to Chumley's place; he didn't know why. No one else visited the flat while the girl was there.'

'Hmm,' said Dawlish. 'It doesn't help much, but it does confirm. I wonder whether there is further news this morning of Simon? Simon, Oroshu, North. Our three possibilities as far as I can see.'

'Oroshu's under lock and key, I expect,' said Beresford, 'and North is probably in Kingdom Come.'

There was a ring at the front door bell, but it proved to be the attendant with the ambulance which had come for Felicity. Dawlish watched her go with mixed feelings. Both men were standing at the window of the flat when they saw a man hurrying beneath the window; they only had a distorted view, for they were looking down on him.

'For us, I wonder?' asked Dawlish, hopefully.

He was at the open door when the visitor hurried up the steps, and drew a sharp breath when he saw that it was North, dishevelled and feverish-eyed, and breathing heavily.

CHAPTER TWENTY-ONE

NEWS ROUND ABOUT

Dawlish stood aside to let the man enter. North waited only for the door to close before gasping out:

'Dawlish, you've got to help me, you've got to!'

Dawlish said sharply: 'What the hell are you doing here? I thought you were under cover? D'you think I want the police after me for sheltering you?'

'I can't help that!' North's voice was high-pitched, almost hysterical. 'I—I've just had a frightful shock, Dawlish, frightful! I went—I went to see Fuelling. I thought he might be able to help us. And he's dead! Shot dead!'

'Ah. So they've killed Fuelling, have they?' Dawlish said.

'Yes, it—it happened early this morning. I don't know

everything, but I managed to have a word with the porter of the flats. The—the police called first, the porter says, and then two Japanese arrived. They killed Fuelling and one of the policemen, and—Dawlish. Dawlish!' North leaned forward, gripping Dawlish's forearms tensely. 'They took away a pile of papers, Fuelling had been keeping records, getting information from the Professor and compiling reports. There isn't any doubt of it, the porter overheard the police talking. That Inspector What's-his-name, Trivett, he was there taking reports from one of the policemen.'

'Munk,' said Dawlish absently. He did not appear to be overwhelmed by the information, and North glared at him impatiently.

'Dawlish, don't take it so damned coolly! Don't you see what it means? Papers have been stolen, information has been taken from the Professor, and Fuelling did it! Fuelling did it, and I'm suspected!'

'Steady,' said Dawlish. 'Everyone connected with the Professor is suspected, no one assumed that it had to be you. There's only Arthurson left, isn't there?' he added, still absently.

'The police seem to be useless!' North cried. 'They're doing all the wrong things, if they get me——'

Dawlish eyed him coldly.

'North, I pity Georgette if she ever marries you. You need guts for this life, and you don't seem to have them. Stop snivelling. You've done nothing but lose your head from the beginning, and given me and the police a dozen reasons for thinking you've been playing a crooked game. For heaven's sake keep a hold on yourself.'

'Try this,' said Beresford consolingly, holding out a whisky-and-soda.

North grabbed the glass, spilt a little, and then drank the rest at a gulp. Beresford eyed him with an admiring surprise, while Dawlish tried to keep his own feeling of contempt from showing in his face. He did not wholly succeed, for as he banged the empty glass down, North muttered:

'It's all very well for you, you're used to this kind of thing. I haven't had any experience before, and the danger to Georgette has almost driven me crazy!' He glared at Dawlish as if he would gladly strike him, his voice rising perceptibly. 'I tell you I don't know what I'm doing or thinking half the time!'

'You're telling me!' said Dawlish unpleasantly. 'What happened after Georgette and I left last night?'

'I hurried out the back way,' North said. 'I thought there'd be a better chance of avoiding the police if I did. I think they would have followed me but there was an explosion nearby, and I managed to slip away in the confusion.'

Dawlish stared at him. 'Nearby?' he echoed.

'What do you say it like that for?' demanded North.

'Are you telling me that you didn't know Number 31 was blown sky-high?' demanded Dawlish, and then watched North's mouth gape open.

'B-blown sky-high?' he muttered. 'But—but we'd all been there, it wasn't five minutes earlier. If we hadn't left when we did we would all have been blown to pieces! Oh God, I can't stand it, someone's trying to kill me, I'll never get away!'

Dawlish snapped: 'Look here, North, stop the melodrama. Why should anyone try to kill you? Why should anyone deliberately make it look as if you're a party to the crimes?'

'Are—are they doing that?' gasped North.

'They most certainly are. You're being fixed for one murder if not more,' Dawlish said remorselessly. 'There must be a reason for it, just as there must be a reason for the attempt to kill Georgette the other day. You two know something, and you haven't come across. It's time you did.'

'I don't, I tell you I don't!' North screamed. 'I've no idea, I don't know anything more than I've told you. I——' He looked imploringly at Beresford. 'Can't I have another drink? That was too weak, it didn't do me any good.'

It was then that the door of Georgette's room opened.

The bandage was still about her neck, and her clothes were crumpled, yet she looked indomitable.

'G-Georgette!' North exclaimed. 'Thank heavens you're safe, I was afraid——'

She looked at him, her eyes hard and frosty.

'The only thing you've been afraid for is your own miserable skin,' she said cuttingly. 'I've heard everything you've

138

said. I don't want to hear it again. Captain Dawlish——' She looked away from North quickly. 'I think it would be better if you told the police that I was here. There's no point in keeping this up any longer.'

North gasped: 'Georgette, listen to me!'

'Not any more,' said Georgette freezingly. 'I've listened to you too long. I should have known better. You were protecting yourself, not me.'

'Georgette!' North's voice rose to a scream. 'It's not true. Last night I was only thinking about you, I wouldn't let you down by coming with Dawlish myself, I left you to him.'

'Knowing you'd be better off without me around.'

Dawlish said, bracingly: 'They're nearly the first words of commonsense I've heard from you, Georgette.'

'You rotten swine!' shouted North. 'Everyone rounds on me, everyone!'

Beresford poured out a stiff dose of whisky.

'Drink this, little man, and pipe down for heaven's sake.' He eyed North with unpretended disgust, watching with some interest the speed with which the whisky was downed.

A ring at the front door bell startled them all.

It was Trivett. Dawlish held out a hand with real pleasure. Suddenly North made a rush for the door.

It took Beresford and Dawlish by surprise. Even Trivett was caught unaware, and more easily because he was dependent on one sound leg and his walking stick. But behind Trivett, on the stairs, was a plain-clothes man who checked the wild rush by promptly putting out a leg. North went sprawling.

Dawlish reached them, hauled North up and marched him back into the room. Trivett, helped to his feet by Beresford, was glowering at the secretary, while Georgette showed a mingling of disgust and alarm.

Dawlish felt sorry for her.

'It wouldn't be a bad idea, Bill,' he said off-handedly, 'if you charged North with assault and sent him to cool his heels. What do you think?'

Trivett gave a quick look at Georgette, and busied himself with the necessary formalities. As the door finally shut on North and his escort she walked unsteadily to a chair and sank into it. She did not cry, nor break down, but the impression she gave was that she could not stand much more.

'Tea, Ted?' Dawlish suggested, while Trivett settled back more comfortably, and prepared to talk.

'A lot of things happened during the night, Pat,' he began.

'I'm not surprised.'

'Fuelling was murdered, with one of our men,' Trivett went on. 'The papers in his room, all taken from Wilson's place, were highly confidential, relating to economic arrangements during and after the war.' He did not glance at Georgette, and Dawlish realised that Trivett was deliberately allowing her to hear what he said.

'There's plenty of evidence in Fuelling's flat to prove that he's working with Simon,' Trivett went on. 'Presumably he was preparing the statement for Simon, when Munk arrived. Then, of course, the Japs. They didn't waste their bullets,' Trivett added abruptly.

'And the presumption is?' asked Dawlish.

'Isn't it obvious? That Simon was having Fuelling's flat watched, and as soon as it was seen that the police were there his men went for the papers.'

'Obviously a man not quite so simple as the nursery rhyme suggests,' said Dawlish drily.

Trivett spoke irritably.

'If the only other copies of the papers were at Portman Square, they were destroyed in the explosion and the fire. That means that Simon has the only ones now available.'

'Arthurson?' murmured Dawlish.

'He was detained late last night, in Manchester,' said Trivett. 'He had no papers of importance with him, only notes for the Conference he was attending. The Conference wasn't a large one, its business was comparatively unimportant—help for some of the occupied countries after the war. When I say unimportant, I mean it affected no present issues.'

'So,' said Dawlish, 'the Japs have the only papers which might be of current importance? Odd how the Japs have been in this show from the start, from Kori Oroshu downwards. Any news from Cranton, Bill?'

'There won't be for several days—if then. It's still touch

140

and go with him.'

'Hmm,' said Dawlish. 'We can't say they weren't thorough.' He looked across at Georgette who was leaning back in her chair, her eyes closed. 'Ted will have the tea ready soon,' he said, 'and if you feel like a snack, we can manage it. Don't say you're not hungry, you didn't have any supper.'

As Beresford entered with the tray, Dawlish saw with approval that he had cut some bread and butter.

Trivett accepted a cup of tea, and drained his cup. As he did so his smile widened.

'Damn you, Pat, you've got an idea up your sleeve. I can see it all over you.'

Dawlish chuckled.

'Well, I think I know most of it, now—but not just why it started when it did. It may have been because the Professor grew suspicious, but I have doubts. It was planned carefully, and no time's been lost. Very little has gone wrong—or so they think.'

'You mean Simon thinks?' Trivett rubbed his chin. 'We haven't got him yet, you know.'

'We will have,' said Dawlish confidently.

Trivett's next question was interrupted by the ringing of the telephone. Hermina Blake was on the line, demanding to know whether she and her Freddie were going to be kept in all the morning. They wanted to go and see the shops.

'You mean you do,' said Dawlish, laughing. 'Well, I don't see why you shouldn't, there's nothing you can usefully do at the moment. Unless,' he added suddenly, 'you'd be a fairy godmother, and take someone else with you.'

'Who?' demanded Hermina suspiciously.

'Just a moment,' said Dawlish, and put a hand over the telephone mouthpiece. 'Georgette, Hermina Blake's in London —remember her?' He did not wait for an answer, but continued: 'You won't want to hang about here all day. A little shop-hunting will do you good. Feel like it?'

Georgette nodded listlessly.

'Good,' said Dawlish, and uncovered the mouthpiece. He arranged for Georgette to be at Piccadilly Circus, outside Swan and Edgar's, in half an hour's time. He warned Hermina that Georgette would be a little on the creased and rumpled side, adding that she would almost certainly need to buy a complete outfit, or as near one as her coupons would permit.

'A new outfit!' Hermina exclaimed excitedly. 'Tell her I think I can rake up a few coupons for her!'

Georgette smiled a little more animatedly at this relayed remark.

'I hadn't thought about clothes,' she said. 'Of course, all mine were destroyed last night.'

'You hadn't thought about *clothes*!' Dawlish was shocked. 'You need a dose of Hermina, she'll put you right. Have you another man outside, Bill?'

'Yes,' said Trivett.

'He'd be useful looking after Georgette and making sure nothing goes wrong,' Dawlish suggested.

Trivett made no comment, and twenty minutes later Georgette left, with the plain-clothes man just behind her. Dawlish was at the telephone, and a moment later called urgently to Trivett:

'For you, Bill. The Yard. Get half a dozen of your best men after Georgette and the Blakes.' He saw Trivett's bewilderment, and added urgently: 'It's vital, Georgette's in real danger.'

Trivett took the telephone, asked for an Inspector Dell, and made the necessary arrangements swiftly. Almost in the same breath as he said 'goodbye' he turned to Dawlish.

'Now perhaps you'll explain these dramatic barkings. What's going to happen to Georgette?'

'She's the only one left,' Dawlish said. 'The only one, don't make any mistake about that. The others are either safely in your hands, dead, or incapacitated.' There was more than a hint of excitement in his eyes as he picked up the telephone again and dialled another number. When an operator answered, he said: 'This is Captain Patrick Dawlish, asking for the Minister for War, please.'

Trivett said: 'You *are* crazy!'

'Does anyone mind if I go back to my unit,' murmured Beresford. 'I don't think I can stand this any longer.'

'Hallo,' said Dawlish into the telephone. 'Good morning,

sir.' He grinned towards Trivett and Beresford, neither of whom had dreamed he would be connected with McKye so quickly, and added: 'May I come to see you, with Chief Inspector Trivett . . . oh, good. I'll be there in twenty minutes.'

He replaced the receiver, slid his hands into his pockets, and said clearly:

'The Minister for War, my sons, was about to telephone me. Morely's there with him now, and he would like to see us within the next half-hour.'

They made their way to Whitehall in comparative silence, only when Beresford was paying the driver did Dawlish say earnestly:

'I think I see it now. Simon J. Simon isn't obviously on the other side, he's working his tortuous way on ours. All the evidence points to that. There's hell to pay at the War office this morning because the Japs took the figures from Fuelling. Fuelling was linked up with Simon, yes, but officially that was all right. He prepared the statement, whatever it was about, and then the Japs lifted it. There's your set-up.'

'I don't believe it!' declared Trivett roundly.

'It's the spring weather,' suggested Beresford.

'Well, wait and see,' declared Dawlish.

They were taken to McKye's office with surprising expeditiousness, conducted by the cold-faced secretary whom Dawlish had first seen at Whitehall. Dawlish entered behind Trivett and Beresford and so was able to hear their exclamations of surprise on seeing Simon J. Simon at the desk with McKye. Sir Archibald Morely was standing with his back to a window.

All three men were grave-faced.

CHAPTER TWENTY-TWO

MOTIVE POWER

Three chairs were already in position for the trio.

'Gentlemen,' said Dawlish, beating McKye to the opening words by a fraction of a second, 'on the whole I don't think I've had a square deal. Nor have the police.'

A faint smile eased the gravity of McKye's expression.

'Don't you, Mr. Dawlish?'

'No,' said Dawlish, 'I've been the Aunt Sally, and Simon's been doing the work. Only,' he added gently, 'some of it escaped him.'

Simon pursed his full lips.

'Captain Dawlish, I did not realise that you——'

'That I had caught on,' Dawlish said. 'I didn't until this morning, but it came on me after a good night's sleep. You'll forgive me, sir,' he added to the Minister blandly, 'for getting the satisfaction of the first blow.'

'Supposing you tell us what you know,' suggested McKye.

'Thanks,' said Dawlish, 'perhaps I should amend that, to "what I *think* I know". Shall we go back to the beginning? Briefly, then, Colonel Cranton advised calling on me; Mr. Simon was against it. When he realised that the Colonel had not been able to make a statement to me, Mr. Simon persuaded you and others to keep me in the dark, but allowed it to be known by the other side that I was working against them. Isn't that so, Mr. Simon?'

Simon nodded.

'The idea, of course, was for me to draw their fire while you did the work. It would have helped had I known.'

'How did you reach that conclusion?' McKye appeared really interested, leaning forward with his chin cupped in his hands.

'Mr. Simon was in it so much, and yet nothing really disastrous followed his operations,' said Dawlish. 'He arranged with Oroshu to detain me, and it was done just violently

144

enough to encourage me to think that I had a justifiable grievance. Miss Deverall was drugged but not harmfully; although the indications all the time was for me to watch Mr. Simon. In short, he had so many opportunities for doing real damage, yet missed them so frequently that I began to wonder whether his part was really what it seemed. So I took a mental exercise in grand strategy, and saw the force of the argument that if the other side concentrated on me, Simon would be in a much better position to work.

'All this,' Dawlish went on, 'sprang from the death of Professor Wilson and the fact that his death created a sudden emergency. I doubted from the first whether the Professor had really left it so late as it appeared before reporting the threats. And,' went on Dawlish with a slow smile which caused a responsive twinkle in McKye's eyes, 'I couldn't understand why I had suddenly been called upon. It wasn't reasonable to believe that in the first few days of the inquiry I would be brought from manoeuvres. At the time I didn't give that as much thought as I might have done, but when I did get to work on it it occurred to me that, some earlier efforts having failed, someone saw the possibility that I would be useful as a diversion. Was I right?'

'Quite right,' McKye said. 'I didn't think you'd see it, Dawlish.'

'Oh, Aunt Sallies become preternaturally sensitive,' Dawlish said airily. 'However, results were wanted, and there's no point in arguing about how they were to be obtained.' He beamed at McKye. 'The readiness with which you cancelled the recall telegram made me quite sure that you knew just why I was wanted here, and since everyone that I knew of was out of action—everyone who knew what Wilson knew, I mean—someone on our side was working under cover. Over a period, Mr. Simon proved to be the only likely man.'

Beresford turned to regard his friend wide-eyed.

'You secretive blighter,' he said, 'you didn't even give me a hint!'

'I've never known you take one,' murmured Dawlish.

Morely said quietly: 'I'm not really surprised that you saw through it, Dawlish, but we're beyond that stage now, and on to the next one. I wonder if——'

'A moment,' Dawlish interrupted. 'I would like to know where Oroshu stands in this.'

Simon said: 'Oroshu has given us a great deal of help in many ways. Unreliable people are often at the Aliens' Club, and we get many snatches of information from Oroshu. You are wondering, of course, why you were knocked out at the Club, and why Miss Deverall was drugged. The purpose was solely to direct your inquiries towards Oroshu, to make the real antagonist believe that you, his main opponent, were working on the wrong lines. You were to suspect both me and Oroshu.'

Dawlish said: 'I'd wondered about that. In my opinion— speaking figuratively, of course—it's been far too complicated, a frontal attack on the enemy would have been more effective.' He beamed. 'Do you know your man, Mr. Simon?'

'No,' said Simon, 'not for certain.'

'Did you know about the Mooneys?'

'I had heard of them. I have no idea who killed them, no real idea who killed Chumley and Breddon, or who staged the accident at Salisbury. You see, Captain Dawlish, you have made one omission. My purpose was less to smash the enemy than to get certain facts at his disposal but not yet sent from the country. These facts concerned economic assistance now being rendered to allied and neutral countries, *and* to occupied countries. We are helping most of them very substantially. Obviously it would be of great assistance to Berlin to know how. Berlin, and to some measure Tokio and Rome, concentrated on obtaining that information. My own task comprised counter espionage, with Colonel Cranton, thus explaining a matter which I believe has mystified you. In short, the connection between an economic matter and the War Office.'

Simon stopped, and McKye went on a little wearily:

'Right, then!' McKye grew more brisk. 'They obtained the information piecemeal, usually from representatives at various conferences. Under cover of the conferences, by the way, meetings of the espionage organisation concerned primarily with the matter under review, met together; you interrupted such a meeting yesterday.'

'I'd guessed that,' Dawlish murmured.

'Right, then!' McKye grew more brisk. 'They obtained the information piecemeal, as I say. Simon discovered just what pieces they had obtained, and Fuelling, who took much work home because he was helping in the counter espionage measures and needed to work unobserved, was finding just how much had been learned. Then Simon went one better, and obtained the actual papers which the enemy had stolen. Fuelling was co-ordinating them and preparing a full report when he was killed. The original documents, in short all the information which the subversive organisation has gathered together over a long period, is now in the hands of the enemy. Just a moment, Dawlish! Other steps have been taken outside of your knowledge. The secretary Arthurson was a traitor, and his conference in Manchester was really a fake, covering enemy activities. It was raided, and its members arrested. From there Simon regained the documents which have since been stolen. For the first time Simon is compelled to admit an *impasse*. But—we *must* get those documents back.'

'Hmm, a spot easier said than done,' mused Dawlish. 'Everyone who might be anyone has been arrested, but still the enemy can find operators.' He leaned back and closed his eyes, the picture of indolence. 'I suppose,' he asked of the ceiling, 'none of you ever thought seriously that Professor Wilson and his daughter could be supplying the information, calling on your help in order to give themselves a cover? Possible, isn't it?' He widened his eyes abruptly and stared at Simon, who leaned forward with his lips slightly parted, a hand clenched above the desk.

'Wilson!' exclaimed Morely. 'But he's dead——'

'His daughter isn't, and what's more her behaviour has been open to doubt from the start. We've all been inclined to think her a victim of circumstances, but guilt would explain many of her contradictions.'

'No, damn it!' exclaimed Beresford. 'You're talking through your hat, Pat.'

'This is no time for sentiment,' said Dawlish sharply.

'It's time for logic,' interrupted Morely, 'and it isn't logical to suggest that she could be involved, or Wilson, when both

147

were crashed in Cranton's car and when on your own evidence she was nearly strangled at Portiman Square.'

Dawlish said: 'The crash can be explained easily enough. At the time the other operatives who engineered it did not know that Wilson *et fille* were involved. The attempted strangling can also be explained. Georgette was in a pretty stew after the death of her father, and once or twice was probably on the point of talking. She might well have threatened to give the whole show away. You'll grant the *possibility* that she might be involved?' Dawlish looked from one man to another, seeing their tension, noting that Morely was the most sceptical.

Simon snapped: 'Where is the girl now?'

'Shopping, probably in Oxford Street,' said Dawlish. 'She's being watched by half a dozen police officers, so she won't get away. Who's coming?'

Because he could not move freely Trivett did not accompany Dawlish, Beresford, Morely and Simon. They crowded into a taxi after Morely had telephoned the Yard to find out where Georgette was, and it was arranged for them to be told while they waited outside a specified store in Oxford Street. On the way little was said, although Morely showed no relaxation from the mood of scepticism with which he had first greeted Dawlish's theory.

Dawlish, however, felt satisfied with progress.

There was much left unexplained, but being human he could not repress a feeling of satisfaction at being called, finally, to play a part other than one of mere diversion. There were many confused thoughts in his mind, but there were two very clear ones.

He wondered how long it would be before he would be able to put them to the test.

A man approached their stationary taxi, and saluted Morely.

'Report from Inspector Dell, sir. Miss Wilson is in Harridges' Tailoring Salon. Second floor, sir.'

'Thanks,' said Morely crisply. 'Tell the driver, Beresford, will you?'

Beresford passed on the message, and in two minutes the

quartette was stepping out of the taxi. They went by the lift, then walked through the first department, a vast *salon* devoted to the sale of women's gowns. The Tailoring Department, Dawlish knew, dealt in ready-made two-pieces and the variety of clothes that women demanded to be tailored. He was the first to see Georgette standing in front of a mirror, examining herself critically.

By her side was Hermina Blake; thoroughly immersed in vicarious pleasure. Some distance away Freddie Blake sat turning the pages of a magazine, looking thoroughly bored.

'Steady a moment,' Dawlish said as Simon and Morely made to show themselves. 'Your fellows should be handy in case of emergency.'

'What emergency can there be?' demanded Morely irritably.

'One never knows,' said Dawlish. 'Nothing in this show has turned out as we expected. Black's white, and white's black—if we believe all we're told.' He beamed at Simon.

'She looks such a damned nice kid!' Beresford murmured. 'I still think you're barking up the wrong tree, Pat.'

'Possibly,' said Dawlish, 'and possibly not. Mr. Simon, I think you owe me a break.'

'In what way?' Simon demanded.

'I want to have a word with Georgette on my own,' Dawlish told him. 'Two minutes will be enough.' Simon nodded reluctantly, while Dawlish gripped Ted's arm. 'You come with me part of the way, old boy.' He strode forward, and when well out of earshot of the other two, said urgently to Beresford: 'There'll be an avalanche of trouble in about three minutes, maybe less. Watch for it.'

'Right,' Beresford said, showing no surprise or hesitation.

With an air of insouciance Dawlish sauntered towards Georgette. She caught sight of him in the mirror, but continued to stare intently at herself, thoroughly immersed in the task of purchasing an outfit. There were limits, he thought, to the normal woman's interest in clothes; Georgette's did not ring really true, for one whose father had so recently died and whose fiancé had proved, she believed, to be a craven.

She swung round at last.

'Hallo, Captain Dawlish! What do you think of this one?'

'Never ask a man, my dear!' exhorted Hermina. 'They know nothing about clothes and yet have so many prejudices. That's an invariable rule of my life, isn't it, Freddie?' Freddie looked up and grunted, while Georgette ignored Hermina and turned about.

Dawlish put his head on one side.

'Yes,' he said. 'Skirt a trifle long perhaps. But you could cut a piece off and save it for patching later.' He looked past her into the mirror, discerning a movement in the doorway. As if by accident, his hand touched his holster.

Suddenly Beresford shouted: 'Look out, Pat, look out!'

On his words Dawlish snatched his gun and jumped forward, arms spread wide. He caught Hermina in his left and Georgette on his right, and crashed with them to the floor. As they fell, a strange noise filled the *salon*, the *tap-tap-tap* more fitting to a battlefield than the saleroom of beautiful clothes. He heard the mirror shatter, then a piece of broken glass buried itself in the padded shoulder of his coat.

He called out to the two women:

'Keep flat, for your lives!'

He saw Beresford firing towards the door. A man holding a tommy-gun collapsed, so that the bullets from the final burst went towards the ceiling. Assistants were screaming, while another spate of bullets from a second machine-gun tore through a row of gaily-coloured frocks, sending a dozen of them to the floor.

Dawlish fired towards a group of armed Japanese and saw three of them fall. Behind them two plain-clothes policemen appeared. The Japs turned, firing point-blank.

Then Dawlish saw a thing that momentarily froze him to the ground. *The remaining Japs were donning gas-masks.*

CHAPTER TWENTY-THREE

CLEAR-OUT OF JAPS

The shooting had stopped momentarily, and Beresford was taking a chance by getting to his feet and rushing towards the little group near the shattered mirror. Freddie had ducked behind a counter, and was now peering over it. Morely was on the floor, a hand feeling his left shoulder. Near him Oinion was crouching warily with an automatic in his hand.

Beresford arrived, and Dawlish snapped trenchantly:

'Gas!'

Beresford unslung his respirator from his shoulder.

'Give this to Georgette.'

He raced for the windows, while Hermina Blake and her husband Freddie reached uncertainly for their civilian gas-masks.

Dawlish wondered whether they could adjust them in time.

Beresford was bellowing for help in opening the windows. Dawlish saw that Georgette knew how to use a service respirator, and then put on his own.

It happened very quickly. A glass container smacked against the mirror and broke. A yellowish cloud escaped from it, and from another which broke near Dawlish's feet. He saw through the mist about him that there were at least a dozen Japanese, all crowding round the door; and he knew that they were there to make sure that no one entered that way until their task was finished.

That task was obvious; it was the complete destruction of the little party in the middle of the room.

A gust of wind swept from the windows, and Dawlish caught a glimpse of Beresford lifting a woman out of one. He remembered that there was a balcony outside, running the whole face of Harridges' building. Beresford lifted another woman out, while from the Japs shooting started again.

Dawlish muttered to Georgette: 'Crawl to the other side of the dressing-cubicle.'

Georgette began to obey, easing herself over the carpet. Hermina followed her example, and Dawlish felt that they were at least safe from the shooting. He followed, with Freddie, firing twice as he did so.

The waves of gas were spreading. He saw a Jap, whose mask had not been securely fitted, begin to cough, doubling up and then falling to the ground. He wondered how many of the police had been affected, and whether any of them would be able to attack the assailants from the rear. His mind was oddly detached as he peered round the broken mirror, then jerked his head back as a bullet ripped towards him.

The Japs were dispersing, creeping round on either side of the *salon*. Their aim was to get into position where they could have a clear view of their targets, and Dawlish knew that it would be fatal if they succeeded. He called to Freddie:

'Can you stop them that side?'

'Try,' Freddie called back, and moved to the other side of the cubicle. Dawlish waited until a man was just within his vision and then fired. The man went down, but another took his place. Dawlish fired again, and with the second casualty the courage of the little men suffered a temporary setback.

In the ensuing pause Dawlish saw Beresford returning from the windows. He was now in clear view of the Japs. Dawlish took a chance and showed himself, emptying the last three bullets from his gun into the group clustering round the door. It gave Beresford respite enough to reach him.

Crouching behind the cubicle, he reloaded his gun.

'Properly prepared, weren't you?' growled Beresford. 'What's to do?'

'Can't decide,' said Dawlish. 'Better see it out here unless anything else develops. Simon's gone, he should bring help. Left his gun with Morely.'

Morely was approaching the counter which gave him more cover, firing as he did so, while from a doorway which Dawlish had not noticed before there came a spatter of bullets towards the Japanese.

'Simon's helpers, probably,' Dawlish muttered. 'I hope the little swine haven't got another surprise cooking.'

Beresford said nothing.

The air was thick with cordite smoke as well as with gas, and there was a constant echoing of shots.

Then Dawlish saw something else being hurled through the air.

He shot the man who tossed it, but was too late to prevent the object from falling. In size not unlike a Mills bomb, it landed ten yards from him, and in a flash he was faced with the need for getting to it and throwing it back, or waiting for the explosion which might be fatal. If he went, he knew that the Japs would have him in easy range.

'Keep flat,' he called, cursing because his voice was muffled by the mask. 'Keep flat!'

There was a sharp *crack*! and then a series of smaller ones. Instantly Dawlish recognised it for what it was, and for the first time since he had seen the gas preparations he felt that there was little hope.

It was a fire-bomb.

The little centres of conflagration were jumping about the carpet, the smell of burning even piercing his respirator. He saw the flames leaping, growing brighter near the rows of clothes, some of which started to go up like tinsel. In a matter of seconds there were a dozen fires in different parts of the salon.

Beresford muttered: 'Retreat, I think.'

'Hold it to the last minute,' cautioned Dawlish. 'They're still waiting to pick us off.'

He could only just see the Japs through the gathering smoke and flames, but he did discern one of them moving on his stomach towards the far end of the counter.

Dawlish fired and missed.

The man disappeared, and Dawlish knew that at any moment he might dodge up to try a chance shot. Morely was nearer him than any of the others, but Morely had not seen him. The A.C. was still sitting against the counter; Dawlish imagined he had been hit both in the shoulder and the leg.

'Getting hot,' Beresford muttered.

He forced a grin, but there was nothing laughable in the situation. The heat was terrific. Hermina was straining at her gas-mask; it would not be long before she took it off.

'Now!' he said after a pause. 'Let's chance it.'

The air coming through the windows was fanning the flames but blowing them towards the door and away from Dawlish and his party. He nodded to Hermina, catching Freddie's eye. Freddie crawled to his wife, and Dawlish was astonished to see him turn his gun in his hand.

Freddie struck Hermina just behind the ear.

She collapsed, no longer straining to get her mask off. Freddie's expression, behind his mask, was surely one of amusement, Dawlish thought. He wasted no time in worrying about that, but motioned to Beresford to give Freddie a hand; Hermina was no light weight.

Together the two men eased her across the carpet. Dawlish felt the heat so great that his own breathing was growing laboured. He knew how strong Hermina's temptation must have been to snatch off her mask. He turned to Georgette.

'Together we go, my girl, and make it snappy.'

She began to crawl in Beresford's wake, Dawlish moving just behind her, to give her protection. A few bullets struck the floor not far away, but he was sure that the Japs were firing for the sake of it; there was little likelihood that they could see their targets.

Painfully crawling, he saw Beresford and Freddie by the window, hauling Hermina to her feet. Laboriously they lifted her out. Another gust of wind swept into the *salon*, making the air clear for a moment before it thickened again.

He heard the ringing of fire-engines and of ambulances, and remembered the scene in Portiman Square. This would not be unlike it. He saw Georgette reach the window, and straighten up.

'Over, quickly,' he said, but his voice was so hoarse that it was unlikely that she heard him. Nevertheless she did what he wanted, climbing over the sill swiftly, maintaining the calm she had shown throughout.

Dawlish turned to watch the scene.

The fire had so good a hold now that he knew it would be impossible to save any of the *salon* from destruction, and there was more than a possibility it would spread to the rooms adjoining. The flames were so fierce and the smoke so thick that all three doorways were hidden, and he had no way of telling whether the Japs remained there, or whether they had managed to get away.

He reached the balcony.

Then, something struck the wall close to his head.

From a window on the other side of Oxford Street he saw a flash of flame. Another bullet struck the wall, a third appeared to touch Georgette's shoulder.

She started, and slipped.

The balcony railing was a low and narrow one. The sharp surprise of the bullet sent her off balance and she toppled sideways. Dawlish shot out a hand and grasped her wrist, straining to pull her back.

Slowly, inch by inch, he managed to pull the girl upright.

She had all but lost consciousness. As she leaned against him Dawlish watched the opposite windows anxiously, afraid of further shooting, but he saw neither the gun nor the man who had used it.

Beresford, quick to see the position, moved up quietly.

With Georgette between them they walked along the balcony until, at the very end, they were helped through a window by half a dozen people.

None of them wore masks.

Dawlish stripped off his own, while a policeman removed Georgette's. She was unsteady, and would have fallen but for the man's hold. Dawlish looked about him urgently.

Morely was there, thank God! A man was bending over him, cutting the shoulder of his coat away. Freddie was demanding a drink, Hermina beside him, still dead to the world. For the first time Dawlish smiled, for Hermina would never know what had struck her, and Freddie would probably treasure the memory for life of, for once, being in a position to stop her prattle.

They were all there, Dawlish thought wearily, except Simon.

Then he saw the man coming in from a door leading to the lifts. He appeared quite unhurt, and came up smiling.

'Ten of them, Dawlish. We have ten of them, and others were in the *salon*, they could not escape.'

155

Dawlish said grimly: 'One of them escaped, or else didn't get here.'

'What is that?' Simon raised his head abruptly.

'A sharp-shooting merchant still operates,' said Dawlish, 'and I don't know whether I, or Georgette Wilson, was his especial target.'

'But Dawlish, the girl of course, she who can tell us so much!' Simon grew positively excited. 'All the time I have been wondering why it should be that the evidence for Chumley's murder and also for Breddon's should point towards her and the Professor. I had started on the wrong foot, I had assumed their innocence and imagined that there was not the slightest doubt that they were sincere. Now—you have explained it. Their guilt gives us the finishing touch.'

'I'm beginning to wonder,' Dawlish said.

'Nonsense, my friend! I have a piece of knowledge which has not reached you. It is this. Wilson had a small cottage from where he doubtless worked. The letters, they were post-marked from Salisbury. His cottage is on the outskirts of the town, a small village near, you understand that? I have arranged for it to be visited.' Simon drew in a deep breath as he turned beaming eyes towards Dawlish. 'I made one big mistake, Captain Dawlish. I disbelieved the stories I had heard of you. I was wrong, I freely admit it. The Professor and Georgette Wilson—it was a stroke of genius to consider them, Dawlish, and your explanation of the reasons for the attacks on one or both of them was superb. You have the mind attuned to matters of this kind, you are wasted in the army. With your permission I shall recommend that you are posted to service with Cranton. I should welcome you as a colleague, welcome you very much indeed.'

'Thanks, but I'm a soldier,' said Dawlish drily. 'When are you going to this Salisbury cottage?'

'Very soon,' said Simon. 'I have little doubt that we will find all that we need there. I am elated,' he went on joyously, 'I have not felt so pleased for a long time. And to think that I owe so much of that to you!'

'Yes, surprising,' said Dawlish sardonically. 'Why didn't we arrange to go to the Salisbury cottage earlier?'

'Because it was most important to get the girl, of course,' answered Simon. 'You hardly need me to answer that question. You are a humorist, yes.' He beamed. 'But you will need refreshment and a clean-up. I am thinking too much of myself and too little of you. What time will you be ready for the journey to Salisbury?'

'In an hour,' Dawlish said.

'Excellent. One hour it shall be. I will meet you at—no, I will call for you at your flat. Meanwhile I know I can safely leave Georgette Wilson in the hands of the police. Do you not also feel the elation of success, Captain Dawlish?'

'I might have done if that johnnie hadn't started shooting,' said Dawlish. 'Ah, there's Trivett.' He saw Trivett limping into the department. Simon whirled about, exclaiming:

'You will explain, Dawlish, please. I must make preparations for this final raid. I will call in one hour. Goodbye for the present.'

'So long,' said Dawlish. 'Hallo, Bill. What are they doing about the fire?'

'You needn't worry about that,' said Trivett. 'There are three engines working outside, and they're bringing a hose through the shop. What's to do?'

Dawlish said: 'We'll get to the flat and talk there. I think we'd better bring Georgette with us.' He glanced towards her, seeing that though she had not fully recovered from her ordeal, she was very much better.

'What happens now?' she demanded. 'The man who shot at us—where is he?'

'We'll learn,' said Dawlish. 'On the whole the results are good, Georgette.'

Trivett, remembering Dawlish's recent theories on the girl, eyed him thoughtfully. He knew the day would never dawn when Dawlish would say all he thought before he had evidence to support it.

They moved off to the flat, where Georgette, thankfully accepting towels, soap and plenty of hot water, shut herself in the bathroom.

Trivett sat on the arm of a chair, looking fixedly at the ferrule of his walking stick.

157

'Well, Pat?' he asked abruptly. 'What's happening with the girl?'

'I think I'll take her down to Salisbury,' said Dawlish, and explained what Simon had told him. 'Ted, you'll go down with Simon when he arrives—all right?'

'I'll buy it,' Beresford said. 'Where's the catch?'

'We don't know, yet,' said Dawlish. 'Bill, will you arrange with the Salisbury people to have this cottage watched, and surrounded. There might be another packet of trouble there, and we mustn't take too many chances.'

'Not take chances!' demanded Trivett with acerbity. 'My God, you've chanced the massacring of the lot of us!'

'Oh no,' said Dawlish. 'I only half expected it. The outstanding problem is, did they want to kill me or were they after Georgette?' He waved a hand. 'We'll know in a few hours, I hope. And now I'm going to wash in the kitchen, there isn't a lot of time to spare. You know Wilson's country address, I take it?'

Trivett nodded.

'Holden Cottage, Branley—it's on the other side of Salisbury. I've never been there, and you'd better get one of the local men to guide you from the town. I'll phone the police,' he added, and stretched out for the telephone.

Beresford accompanied Dawlish to the kitchen, and asked while Dawlish was washing:

'Why don't I come with you, Pat?'

'Someone's got to keep Simon happy,' Dawlish said. 'The theory is that the damning documents will be at the cottage. If they are, it bears out the Professor–Georgette theory. If they're not——'

'You don't seriously doubt that now, do you?' exclaimed Beresford. 'Damn it, I thought you'd convinced everybody!'

'I believe I did!' exclaimed Dawlish. 'Hand me a towel, old son, and hold your curiosity back for a few hours longer. This has been a tortuous business, but it will end, you know. I wonder——' He paused, and then went on with a note of urgency: 'Ask Trivett to arrange for a plane to pick Georgette and me up at Heston, will you? If he can't, to phone McKye. Hurry, my son, speed counts!'

158

'There are times when I have grave doubts of your sanity,' admitted Beresford, making for the door. 'Must you act like a grasshopper?'

As he went to the bedroom Dawlish heard Trivett saying that it would probably be quicker to arrange for the plane through McKye, but what the devil was Dawlish playing at?

'A new craze,' said Beresford. 'They take him this way, you ought to know that by now.'

Dawlish grinned to himself as he finished dressing. That done, he joined Georgette. There was a hint of excitement in her eyes.

'What's the next step?' she asked.

'A little trip by aeroplane, and then probably some unpleasant surprises,' he told her.

An hour later Dawlish and Georgette boarded a small R.A.F. aeroplane. They had left London far behind them, and were halfway to Salisbury before Dawlish said soberly:

'Georgette, how long had you suspected your father of treating with the enemy?'

CHAPTER TWENTY-FOUR

COTTAGE NEAR SALISBURY

Until Dawlish spoke, Georgette had been looking out of the window and obviously enjoying the flight.

At that moment a small cloud passed beneath them and the sun, so that the cabin was plunged in shadow. It gave added effect to the sudden alarm in in Georgette's eyes.

'I'll have to know,' Dawlish said simply.

She did not speak for several seconds. When she did it was in a voice which the roaring of the single engine made almost inaudible. Dawlish leaned forward, just able to catch her words.

'How did you know? How *could* you know?'

Dawlish said: 'Your manner, Georgette. Shock, yes, but there was something else. You were so very anxious to make it clear that your father had told the authorities. Afterwards, I wondered why. Then there came another question. Why did you visit Chumley after a telephone call, when you refused to go when he wrote to you? I wondered what had made you change your mind. I gathered you were really attached to your father, yet some of the time you were elated, as if with good news. Why was it, Georgette?'

She eyed him uncertainly: he could understand that she did not known how to begin, that she had been taken completely by surprise at the revelation of his suspicions.

Then slowly: 'I've been afraid for a long time that he was a spy. Gerry North—thought so too. We were worried to distraction, but couldn't prove his guilt or innocence, all we found out was that there *was* fifth column work going on at the house. Then there came the threatening letter, and I opened it. I thought that behind it there was the knowledge that Father was a spy, that he would obey because he was afraid of being given away.'

She paused, and Dawlish nodded without speaking.

'When he decided to tell Breddon, I was relieved, I thought it suggested that he wasn't guilty and wasn't afraid of an inquiry. Then we had the journey down to Salisbury. Before we left I'd seen Gerry. He'd found some papers in Father's study, making it look almost certain that he *was* spying, and in touch with Germany. Then came the accident. I—I thought it was against Cranton, I didn't think it was meant for Father and me. But he was dead, whatever happened no further harm could come to him. But it was a horrible thought that he was a spy. I didn't know where I was, nor what I was doing. I just had to get away. The only friend I thought could help me was Gerry.'

Dawlish nodded, and she paused for a moment.

'Getting home was a miserable journey,' she went on, 'but then I saw Gerry and he told me that the real spy was probably Arthurson, and we had a long talk about it. I didn't mind who it was provided it wasn't Father. Then Chumley rang me

160

up. He told me he had some information about Father that he knew I would like to hear. That's why I went to Chelsea,' she added simply.

There was another pause while the plane roared on through the blue skies, and the green countryside spread out beneath them.

Then Georgette went on: 'Chumley told me that Father had been under suspicion for some time, but that evidence recently received proved that he was innocent. I—I was in the seventh heaven. His memory was clear. Oh, you can't know what relief I felt!'

'Did Chumley tell you what he had discovered, and who he suspected?'

'No,' said Georgette. 'He told me I needn't worry about Father. He—he was interested in me, I think he really wanted to see me often.' She paused. 'He was a dear,' she added softly, 'but twice my age. And there was Gerry——'

'Yes,' said Dawlish. 'There was Gerry. You told him what Chumley had told you?'

'But of course I did. He was as pleased as I was—or I thought so. Then we got back to Portiman Square and some-one telephoned him. I don't know who it was, but it scared him, and he started drinking. He always drank too much,' she said slowly. 'If it hadn't been for that he would have been all right. I made him tell me what was the matter. He said that both of us were suspected by the police, and everything you said confirmed it. I wasn't quite myself, and he was excited with the whisky. Does that explain enough, Captain Dawlish?'

Dawlish said: 'I think it does, Georgette.'

But he did not think she had told all the truth.

There was little time for further talk, however. The aero-plane was rapidly losing height, and soon they were taxi-ing across the landing field. Something of the constraint with which she had considered him before had returned when Georgette spoke again.

'Why do you have to be so mysterious?' Her voice was sharp.

'In what way?'

'You're taking me to the cottage, aren't you?'

'That is the idea, yes.'

'Was there any need to keep it from me until we reached here?' Her hands were clenched tightly by her side. 'I thought you trusted me?'

'I can't afford to trust anyone, Georgette, but I'm well disposed towards you, if that's what you're driving at. We've come to Salisbury because others, at my suggestion, are going to visit Holden Cottage. I wanted to get there first. I allowed them to think that I suspected you of double-dealing. They're coming to find the evidence at the cottage. Is there any?'

She said tensely: 'Not to my knowledge.'

'Then you should feel safe,' Dawlish said.

'You heard what I told you about my father,' Georgette said coldly. 'Why didn't you tell me then that we'd know sooner or later, that you were bringing me here to find out? Why can't you act openly with me?'

'Some folk would say I'm taking a whale of a chance with you,' retorted Dawlish. He hailed a passing taxi, directed the driver to Holden Cottage, and then helped Georgette in. They drove in silence until they reached the outskirts of a straggling village. On the green were parked a dozen army transport cars, lined up and covered with camouflage netting. The cabby skirted these, and then pulled up outside a larger house than Dawlish had expected.

Holden Cottage had little to recommend it from the picturesque point of view. It was a Victorian building, more in keeping with London streets than the green Wiltshire countryside.

There was an atmosphere of dilapidation about the grounds, and even the house itself.

'Did you come here often?' asked Dawlish.

'No, not very.' Georgette's manner remained cold and distant as he dismissed the cabby.

'Have you a key?'

'Yes.' Georgette opened her bag. Her hand flashed out as she turned swiftly, pointing a small automatic at Dawlish's chest. 'Don't move!' she snapped. 'Don't move!'

Dawlish stared into Georgette's eyes, reading determination in them, and something else; a tinge of fear, perhaps, of uncer-

tainty, despite her weapon. She kept the muzzle steady, however, and her finger on the trigger.

'So that's it,' Dawlish said at last.

'You asked for it!' she flared back. 'You've done everything
you could against me and my father! If you move I'll shoot
you!' She groped for the bell with her free hand, and tugged.

After a pause, while they stared at each other, Georgette's
grip on her gun a little too tight for Dawlish's liking, there
were footsteps in the hall. The door opened and an old man
appeared. He drew up sharply on sight of the girl's back
turned towards him, and Dawlish's grim face.

'It's all right, Rogers,' Georgette said. 'Don't let this man
scare you. Go on,' she snapped to Dawlish, motioning to the
door with the gun.

Quietly Dawlish went forward, making no effort to rob her
of the gun or to outwit her. He judged that the servant was
nervous, noticing the man's unsteady hands.

The girl followed him into the hall.

'Go upstairs,' Georgette told him. 'Turn your back on me.'

Again Dawlish obeyed, creating the impression that he was
so taken by surprise that there was nothing he could do or
say.

'Up the next flight,' Georgette said when they reached a
landing. 'Don't make any mistakes, Dawlish.'

In front of her Dawlish smiled, although she could not see
it. He turned right towards the next flight of stairs when she
reached the landing. A glance over his shoulder told him that
she had the gun carefully pointing towards his back. It also
showed him that he could return to the first flight of stairs
safely enough with a single leap.

He put a hand on the banister rail casually, tightened his
grip, and vaulted over.

The move took Georgette so completely by surprise that she
only uttered a sharp exclamation. Dawlish landed while Georgette swivelled about, but she was too late to prevent him from
stretching out and grabbing her right ankle. She fell heavily,
and the automatic slipped from her grasp.

It fell close to Dawlish's hand, and he picked it up, raising
one eyebrow above the other as he turned to Rogers, who was

cowering on the stairs.

'Up, old one,' Dawlish said. 'Don't make any mistake, I'm more used to firearms than Miss Wilson.' He let Rogers pass him until he had both Georgette and the servant covered.

'A few bruises here and there can't be helped,' Dawlish said easily, as she clambered to her feet. 'You have to expect it in a rough and tumble, Georgette, you shouldn't start these things without weighing them up beforehand. Go on to the room where you were going to take me. Don't let's waste time.'

She stared at him white-faced, then turned abruptly and continued up the stairs. Dawlish was smiling a little to himself, and even began to hum. Rogers's legs were unsteady as they reached another landing.

There was only one room on this floor, Dawlish noted; Georgette could not deceive him, and she would know it.

By the door she stopped, hesitating.

'Inside,' urged Dawlish. 'I'm waiting to go in.'

She drew a deep breath, then tapped on the door and opened it. There was a movement from within, and an oldish man's voice exclaimed:

'Why, Georgette! My dear, I didn't expect you today!'

'Nor me, I fancy,' said Dawlish, looking into the startled eyes of a grey-haired man who peered at him over the girl's shoulder. 'Good afternoon, Professor. How are you getting on?'

CHAPTER TWENTY-FIVE

CAUTIOUS CALLER

The old man continued to stare at him, eyes wide with alarm. Georgette turned sharply, and but for the gun might have thrown herself at Dawlish.

'You brute!' she shouted. 'You beast, you knew all along!'

Dawlish said quietly: 'No, Georgette, I only realised it in the plane. *You* knew it all along, my dear, while you played

164

Old Harry with me and the police. We had your word for it that he was dead, no one else's. Just what is the idea, Professor?'

Dawlish had only half-suspected this development, and now, seeing Wilson before him, proved quite a shock. He judged the man to be at a high mental stretch, while he believed that Georgette's knowledge that her father was alive explained all her differing moods and tempers.

'Georgette, who is this man?' Wilson's voice was unsteady but he continued to eye Dawlish evenly, showing no signs of immediate collapse.

'Captain Dawlish, at your service,' said Dawlish. 'At a rough guess I'd say we have half an hour before we're interrupted. Georgette, you knew all along that the man with you in the car crash wasn't your father. Isn't that so?'

'Supposing it is?' Her voice was pitched high.

'Supposing we have no more beating about the bush,' said Dawlish sharply. 'You were prevailed on to pretend to Colonel Cranton that it was. You, Professor, were prevailed upon to come here in hiding. Who frightened you? Who threatened you?'

Georgette burst out: 'Those damnable letters! And there were attacks on him. We were both scared, we had to do something. So he came to hide here, and I pretended that someone else was him. I didn't know there was going to be an accident! I'd no idea what was going to happen!' There was agony in her voice. 'You won't believe me, why should you? But it's the truth.'

Dawlish said more easily: 'But I *can* believe it, Georgette. You made the foolish mistake of trying to deceive the authorities, that's where you went wrong. It just doesn't work. Your father was scared enough to hide, and actually did leave for the country. North didn't lie there, anyhow. And someone convinced you that your father was a spy, and thus inspired you to act as you did. Chumley wanted to know whether your father was dead or not, didn't he?'

Georgette said in a muffled voice: 'You seem to know everything. Why waste time in questions?'

'Do stop being obstructive,' said Dawlish wearily. 'You've

dug a pit deep enough for both of you to be buried in. Have the good sense now to help, rather than hinder. You were convinced he was a spy, you were prepared to do everything you could to prevent him from being caught. Chumley suspected the truth. Breddon would have done, too, that's why he was killed, you know. Fuelling, also. Arthurson didn't know, because he was in Manchester, but North knew. Isn't that so?'

Georgette muttered: 'Yes, yes. Father——'

Wilson was looking at her wide-eyed. Dawlish believed that the tone of surprise in his voice was genuine.

'Georgette, my dear! You thought I would act against my country! What on earth possessed you?'

Georgette said: 'Dad! Tell me. Is it a lie?' Her hands went out towards her father, her eyes alight with a sudden hope.

'Of course it's a lie!' Wilson said emphatically. 'I was nervous, yes. I preferred to come here to rest for a while, I had no idea that you had any other thought in mind. I can't believe it, Georgette, I can't credit that your faith in me would be so weak.'

Dawlish said: 'She was convinced by plausible enough arguments, Professor, from a man she believed she could trust. From North, in fact. Georgette—it was North who told you that he was a spy, wasn't it? North who put you up to everything? You told him what Chumley asked, and he went out again after seeing you home from the Chumley discussion. North slipped back to Chumley, told him he had information, and drugged his drink. North knew about Breddon, was aware that Breddon could have told the truth about your father and would have recognised that the dead man was someone else. So North killed him, too. Oh, not altogether on his own,' Dawlish added abruptly. 'He was one of many. I know the others.'

'I—I thought he was sincere, I thought he was frightened because he had helped father,' Georgette said, her voice unsteady.

'North was the real spy in the household,' Dawlish repeated while Wilson stared from one to the other as if trying to understand the talk which was going on over his head. 'He pretended to be a drunk and a coward, but he was cunning enough. He's in prison now, thinking he's safe except for a minor charge. He'll have a shock. And he's not the only one,' Dawlish added. 'I think, Georgette, we'd better stop talking now, I'm expecting visitors.'

'Who else is coming?' Georgette demanded. 'Oh, I don't know what to say, or to think, I've been——'

'Steady, please!' implored Dawlish, and the sharpness of his voice silenced her. 'Now, we've got to act. Beresford and Simon should be here within an hour or two, but I expect others before them. What's the best window for looking into the grounds?'

'This room has two,' Wilson said gravely. 'I will not try to understand what has been said, but if I can be of assistance, please command me.'

'If you and Georgette watch from that window,' Dawlish nodded his head towards the window nearer Wilson, 'I'll see what there is to be seen from this one.'

'Is—is there anything I can do, sir?' The servant spoke nervously.

'Just stand by,' said Dawlish.

He pulled a chair towards the window and rested on the back of it while he surveyed the grounds of the cottage. He was turning over the final story in his mind.

North was the renegade as far as the Wilsons were concerned; but North, clever and cunning though he had been, was not the man to be able to direct such operations on his own. There must be someone else behind him, someone even more dangerous.

Then Georgette exclaimed: 'What's that? Look there!'

Dawlish was at her side in a trice, and all four of them peered in the direction of Georgette's pointing finger. They saw a man break from the shrubbery, stand for a second watching Holden Cottage, and then approach it.

Georgette whispered: 'Is that who you expected?'

'Probably,' Dawlish said. He rested a hand on Georgette's shoulder. 'I want you to stay here, please. You, and your father and Rogers. If you want to see your story substantiated, don't leave the room until I call for you.'

Dawlish turned and left the room, going downstairs at speed. He reached the landing, judging that from here he could get a clear view of the hall, and the passage alongside the stairs. He saw that all but two of the doors within sight were ajar, a satisfying fact.

He waited tensely, with a hand on his gun.

He heard a faint noise, suggesting that the intruder was trying to find the easiest window to force. Silence followed, and then a scratching sound from another room. A sharper noise and then a decided squeak told Dawlish that the man had pushed a window up. The sound came from a room near the foot of the stairs, and Dawlish went down, reaching the door which was ajar.

He peered through.

A man whom Dawlish had never seen before was putting his leg over the sill. In a moment he was standing silently by the open window. In his left hand there was an automatic. Motionless, he appeared to listen, then cautiously approached the door. Dawlish slipped into the next room swiftly.

The intruder's footsteps made no sound.

Dawlish saw him reach the hall, hesitate, and then make for the stairs. Dawlish waited until he was halfway up, and then followed.

On the landing the man paused again.

Then he went along the passage, opened a door and went in, leaving the door ajar. It was a bedroom. Dawlish widened the gap a few inches, while the intruder approached the bed, and flung back a corner of the mattress. Putting the automatic in one pocket he withdrew from another a large, sealed envelope.

He pushed it beneath the mattress and was about to let the corner fall down again when Dawlish said pleasantly:

'Good evening. Can I help you?'

The man swung round so abruptly that he lost his balance. He tried to get his automatic from his pocket but had no chance. Dawlish did not need to draw his gun, but reached the man and disarmed him quickly.

'So, the papers are planted,' Dawlish said. 'Do you know, there have been things in this show too naïve for words. Do I look quite such a fool as all that?'

The man said nothing.

'No,' mused Dawlish. 'At the moment, of course, you might

not think so. Others, I hope, will agree with you before long. What time do you expect them?'

'I—I don't know what you mean!'

'Too bad,' murmured Dawlish. 'I'll explain as the evening wears on, but for the moment I think you'd be better out of action.' He struck the man sharply, easing him to the floor.

Dawlish thought: the Professor would be shocked at such violence. Perhaps he shouldn't know. He hesitated, then reached a rapid decision, taking off the man's tie and securing his wrists before finding another tie in a dressing-table drawer and binding his ankles. That done, he lifted the man and carried him downstairs.

There was a capacious hall-seat, with arms; Dawlish put the man on it, then forced a small handkerchief into his mouth and tied another about it to make sure he could not shout.

Standing back he surveyed his handiwork.

'You'll do, my son. I wonder if——'

He stopped abruptly.

There was a sound outside, and he did not doubt what it was. The driver of a car was changing gear at the far end of the drive. By the time Dawlish had reached a window he was already slowing down.

Beresford was at the wheel, Simon sitting next to him.

Dawlish waited while the others reached the porch. The bell clanged, then echoed away into silence. It rang again. Dawlish heard a mutter of voices, Beresford's predominating.

Another pause, and then an exclamation. They had discovered that the front door was not locked. It squeaked as they pushed it open.

Dawlish, standing by the door of the lounge, was able to see Simon, who entered first. He watched Simon closely until the man stopped in his tracks, staring at the man who lay bound and gagged.

The somewhat complacent expression on his face faded, followed by one of a malignance Dawlish had rarely seen. In that instant, Dawlish knew that his suspicions, kept so rigidly to himself, were justified. He saw Simon flash his hand to his coat pocket, but before it reappeared Dawlish stepped into sight, his heavy revolver covering Simon.

'The game's up, I think.' He sounded bored, and ignored Beresford's stare of sheer bewilderment. 'The planting of evidence didn't quite come off, Simon. Your man was just a bit clumsy, I'm afraid.'

Then Simon, fury choking him, lifted his gun.

CHAPTER TWENTY-SIX

WHEELS WITHIN WHEELS

Dawlish fired first.

His bullet struck Simon's wrist. On the same instant Beresford flung out an arm, buffeting Simon to one side. The man struck the wall and slumped slowly downwards.

'Pat, what the hell is this?' Beresford's bewildered bellow filled the hall. 'Why the devil didn't you warn me?'

'To warn you would be to warn Simon,' Dawlish said sombrely. 'I thought this the best way, Ted. It's been a foul business, and I wanted Simon to show himself in his true colours.'

'But——' began Beresford.

'No buts,' implored Dawlish. 'The facts are these, Ted. Simon's been working plots within plots, using his position on Cranton's Secret Service staff to get information he could pass on to his real master in Tokio. Little of what he said earlier appealed to me, everything was too tortuous. He had McKye with him because he was recommended by Cranton, he pulled the strings and the marionettes worked. I didn't like being a marionette.'

'But how could you know?' Beresford almost howled.

'Simon left Harridges pretty smartly before the real trouble started. He was still missing when Georgette and I were fired at. He returned, and I trotted out further suspicions of Georgette's part in the affair. He jumped at it, I saw him jumping,

170

he has a naïveté in some things that makes me gasp. I could almost see his mind working. He proposed to plant papers here which would damn Wilson and his daughter, and clear the case beyond all reasonable doubt. Eh, Simon?'

Simon glared up at him, but said nothing.

'He wanted Georgette killed at all costs,' Dawlish said, 'because she could tell the truth about her father. He had to prevent that from happening, but Georgette always just slipped out of the net. He tried to blow her up, with me, in Portiman Square. North, who worked for him, had the whole house mined to go off a few seconds after he had left it. That made it look as if the crooks wanted to get him as well as Georgette. All the time Georgette, while alive, was a constant danger to Simon. When he failed to kill her he jumped at the chance of incriminating her and her father. The fact that Wilson was alive wouldn't have mattered then.'

Beresford stared.

'The Professor,' he muttered. 'Not dead?'

'Very much alive,' Dawlish assured him, 'and I fancy very anxious to have an explanation of what's being happening.'

'Where is he?' asked Beresford faintly.

'Upstairs, with Georgette,' said Dawlish. 'I'll go and see him. You might stand on the porch and bellow for the police, they should be around by now.'

They arrived before he left the hall, summoned by the shooting which they had heard from the fields beyond Holden Cottage. Superintendent Fowler was with them, and showed no reluctance to collect Simon and his accomplice and see them safely delivered to London.

Dawlish and Beresford went upstairs together.

Georgette and her father, with Rogers shaking in the background, were waiting anxiously to hear what had happened.

It took Dawlish a long time to tell them.

Finally:

'In its essence, Professor, the plot was the simple one of finding what means of communication the country has with the Occupied Countries, what kind of supplies are being sent "underground", and what kind of espionage system we have in Europe. Your Conferences were ideal covers, a number of the economists concerned being spies. Simon, *persona grata* with Colonel Cranton, was thus able to do more or less what he liked, and to explain many queer things away.

'But Cranton had to hear of it at last; as soon, in fact, as you told Breddon of the threatening letters. You were suspected of discovering what happened, and so had to be got rid of. Simon moved swiftly, seeing the opportunity of proving that you were the spy and working on that basis through North. You were persuaded to come here, and to allow someone else to interview Cranton. Thereafter the world believed you dead; and when it was discovered that you were actually alive, the case would be "proved" against you. But it had to remain in abeyance until Simon had all the information that he wanted. Because of that, Georgette was the weak link, and North did all he could to incriminate her, while frightening her into keeping silent. You can see that?'

'All too clearly,' admitted the Professor.

'Cranton acted on Simon's suggestion to bring in someone else, and I was chosen. Then Simon made sure that I went after him, knowing that he could eventually explain himself. He went to incredible lengths to get himself suspected by me, even planting a nurse in my flat and getting her to telephone to the Aliens' Club with a faked message for Simon.' Dawlish smiled. 'This is rather like talking to myself,' and added: 'Simon wanted Oroshu suspected as a foil to himself. To heighten suspicion he had two of his agents, the Mooneys, brought to the Aliens' Club and murdered there. Yes,' Dawlish added slowly, 'he was a crafty chap, our Simon J. Simon. A brilliant mind, but like most Orientals a shade too tortuous.'

'Is he an Oriental?' Beresford demanded.

'I'm going to be very surprised if he isn't,' said Dawlish. 'He had an answer for everything, he had me shanghaied and released, he drugged Felicity, doing both things to make it seem as if he was not really deadly, to lend colour to his "real" identity. I fell for that once,' Dawlish added wryly.

'You said Oroshu was being put up as a foil,' objected Beresford.

'He was. Oroshu worked for Simon and Cranton, and Simon gave him the instructions to put me out; that's why

172

Oroshu was so blandly confident that I could not make trouble for him. Afterwards Simon would just deny it and he would be believed and Oroshu convicted. All of this,' Dawlish added amiably, 'is what Trivett would call guesswork, but I have little doubt that North will turn King's Evidence.'

North did, breaking down completely when he realised how thoroughly the organisation was smashed.

A little more than three months later, Dawlish was granted forty-eight hours leave. He spent it in Salisbury, since he was stationed near and Felicity could get there easily. Beresford also managed to get away, but Tim Jeremy had to satisfy himself with a trunk call from the North, where he was stationed; Tim, as well as Felicity, had recovered completely.

There had been many conferences.

Cranton had recovered, Trivett, Morely and McKye had heard first Dawlish's outline and then North's corroboration. As Dawlish put it there had been much back-patting all round, even from Sergeant Munk, who had declared it had been a smart job, as good as he could have done himself.

In the lounge of the White Hart, Felicity smiled at Dawlish a little ruefully.

'It's really the kind of work you should be doing all the time, darling. Why don't you apply for a transfer? I'll be good.'

'Great Scott, no!' exclaimed Dawlish. 'Not my normal job at all, sweetheart, my mind only works in snatches, and likes long spells of tranquillity in between. Give me the simple life every time. Ted, catch the porter's eye and order more beer, will you? It's thirsty work, reminiscing.'

THE END

A SELECTION OF FINE READING AVAILABLE IN CORGI BOOKS

Novels

☐ 552 08651 7   THE HAND REARED BOY   *Brian W Aldiss* 35p
☐ 552 09018 2   A SOLDIER ERECT   *Brian W. Aldiss* 35p
☐ 552 09274 6   A KIND OF LOVING   *Stan Barstow* 40p
☐ 552 09156 1   THE EXORCIST   *William Peter Blatty* 40p
☐ 552 09376 9   TREAD SOFTLY IN THIS PLACE   *Brian Cleeve* 40p
☐ 552 09217 7   THE DWELLING PLACE   *Catherine Cookson* 45p
☐ 552 09381 1   FEATHERS IN THE FIRE   *Catherine Cookson* 35p
☐ 552 09380 7   THE ORDEAL OF RUNNING STANDING   *Thomas Fall* 40p
☐ 552 09174 X   A CHEMICAL ROMANCE   *Jenny Fabian* 35p
☐ 552 09303 3   BLACKSTONE   *Richard Falkirk* 35p
☐ 552 09121 9   THE DAY OF THE JACKAL   *Frederick Forsyth* 50p
☐ 552 09158 8   THE GOD BENEATH THE SEA   *L. Garfield & E. Blishen* 30p
☐ 552 09125 6   CATCH 22   *Joseph Heller* 40p
☐ 552 09279 7   STEAMBOAT GOTHIC   *Frances Parkinson Keyes* 50p
☐ 552 09379 3   LARRY VINCENT   *Frances Parkinson Keyes* 40p
☐ 552 09302 5   SITKA   *Louis L'Amour* 40p
☐ 552 09304 1   ESTHER   *Norah Lofts* 30p
☐ 552 09364 5   DRUMS ALONG THE KHYBER   *Duncan MacNeil* 35p
☐ 552 09394 7   JEREMY   *John Minahan* 30p
☐ 552 09256 8   THE LOTUS AND THE WIND   *John Masters* 40p
☐ 552 09240 1   THE DRIFTERS   *James A. Michener* 75p
☐ 552 09378 5   THE HARVEST BURNS   *Helga Moray* 35p
☐ 552 09358 0   LOLITA   *Vladimir Nabokov* 40p
☐ 552 09306 8   THE HIGH ROOF   *Joy Packer* 40p
☐ 552 09140 5   SARAH WHITMAN   *Diane Pearson* 35p
☐ 552 09377 7   GENTLE GREAVES   *Ernest Raymond* 75p
☐ 552 08930 3   STORY OF O   *Pauline Reage* 50p
☐ 552 08597 9   PORTNOY'S COMPLAINT   *Philip Roth* 40p
☐ 552 08372 0   LAST EXIT TO BROOKLYN   *Hubert Selby Jr.* 50p
☐ 552 07807 7   VALLEY OF THE DOLLS   *Jacqueline Susann* 40p
☐ 552 08523 5   THE LOVE MACHINE   *Jacqueline Susann* 40p
☐ 552 08384 4   EXODUS   *Leon Uris* 50p
☐ 552 08481 6   FOREVER AMBER Vol. 1   *Kathleen Winsor* 40p
☐ 552 08482 4   FOREVER AMBER Vol. 2   *Kathleen Winsor* 40p

War

☐ 552 09369 6   THE BRAVE WHITE FLAG   *James Allen Ford* 35p
☐ 552 09383 1   DANGEROUS TRADE   *Gilbert Hackforth-Jones* 30p
☐ 552 08874 9   SS GENERAL   *Sven Hassel* 35p
☐ 552 09178 2   REIGN OF HELL   *Sven Hassel* 35p
☐ 552 09368 8   THREE CAME HOME   *Agnes Keith* 35p

A SELECTION OF FINE READING AVAILABLE IN CORGI BOOKS

War (*contd.*)

☐ 552 09324 6   **FIGHTER EXPLOITS (illustrated)**   *Edward H. Sims* 40p
☐ 552 08986 9   **DUEL OF THE EAGLES (illustrated)**   *Peter Townsend* 50p
☐ 552 09367 X   **SLAVES OF THE SON OF HEAVEN**   *R. H. Whitecross* 35p
☐ 552 09382 3   **FLAME THROWER**   *Andrew Wilson* 35p

Romance

☐ 552 09208 8   **BRIDAL ARRAY**   *Elizabeth Cadell* 30p
☐ 552 09329 7   **CONSIDER THE LILIES**   *Elizabeth Cadell* 30p
☐ 552 09417 X   **THE NIGHT PEOPLE**   *Kate Norway* 30p
☐ 552 09312 2   **NO SINGLE STAR**   *Alex Stuart* 30p
☐ 552 09389 0   **LIFE IS THE DESTINY**   *Alex Stuart* 30p

Science Fiction

☐ 552 09237 1   **FANTASTIC VOYAGE**   *Isaac Asimov* 35p
☐ 552 09289 4   **STAR TREK 8**   *James Blish* 30p
☐ 552 09333 5   **THE GOLDEN APPLES OF THE SUN**   *Ray Bradbury* 35p
☐ 552 09313 0   **NEW WRITINGS IN S.F. 21**   ed. *John Carnell* 35p
☐ 552 09334 5   **THE MENACE FROM EARTH**   *Robert A. Heinlein* 53p

General

☐ 552 09332 7   **GO ASK ALICE**   *Anonymous* 30p
☐ 552 09292 4   **LOVE, LIFE AND SEX**   *Barbara Cartland* 35p
☐ 552 09185 5   **THE FUNDAMENTALS OF SEX (illustrated)**
     Dr. Philip Cauthery & Dr. Martin Cole 50p
☐ 552 09392 0   **THE MYSTERIOUS UNKNOWN (illustrated)**
     Robert Charroux 50p
☐ 552 09151 0   **THE DRAGON AND THE PHOENIX**   *Eric Chou* 50p
☐ 552 08800 5   **CHARIOTS OF THE GODS? (illustrated)** *Erich von Daniken* 35p
☐ 552 09073 2   **RETURN TO THE STARS (illustrated)**   *Erich von Daniken* 40p
☐ 552 09331 9   **OPERATION RHINO (illustrated)**   *John Gordon Davis* 40p
☐ 552 07400 4   **MY LIFE AND LOVES**   *Frank Harris* 65p
☐ 552 98748 4   **MAKING LOVE (Photographs)**   *Walter Hartford* 85p
☐ 552 09062 X   **THE SENSUOUS MAN**   *'M'* 35p
☐ 552 09293 2   **GOLF'S WINNING STROKE: PUTTING (illustrated)**
     Tom Michael 50p
☐ 552 09290 8   **INTIMATE BEHAVIOUR**   *Desmond Morris* 40p
☐ 552 08010 1   **THE NAKED APE**   *Desmond Morris* 30p
☐ 552 09232 0   **SECRET OF THE ANDES**   *Brother Philip* 30p
☐ 552 09390 4   **CANDLELIGHT**   *T. Lobsang Rampa* 35p
☐ 552 09266 5   **ANY WOMAN CAN**   *David R. Reuben M.D.* 50p
☐ 552 09044 1   **SEX ENERGY**   *Robert S. de Ropp* 35p
☐ 552 09250 9   **THE MANIPULATED MAN**   *Esther Vilar* 35p

A SELECTION OF FINE READING AVAILABLE IN CORGI BOOKS